THE MAGNIFICENT PIGLETS OF PIGLETSVILLE

OUR PRESENT-DAY PLIGHT WRAPPED IN A FAIRYTALE

GREG SCHLUETER

Squigglesprout

TROTTERS TOAST!
THE MAGNIFICENT PIGLETS OF PIGLETSVILLE

"A literary masterpiece that transcends genres, weaving a tapestry of wisdom and imagination. An instant classic!"

- Truffle Snoutworthy, *New Pork Times*

"A riveting tale that plunges readers into the heart of Pigletsville, where heroes rise from the unlikeliest places. Unputdownable!"

- Ollie Sizzlehooves, *Porcine Gazette*

"An allegory for our times, brilliantly crafted to illuminate the choices we face. A triumph of storytelling!"

- Hammy Baconington, *The National Oinkquirer*

"In a world where whimsy meets profound insight, this story takes us on a journey of resilience, friendship, and the transformative power of identity. Simply magical!"

- Gruntilda Swirlytail, *Snout Street Journal*

"A symphony of words and imagination. The characters are vivid, the plot enthralling. A literary feast for the soul!"

- Beatrice Hogsbottom, *The Literary Trough Review*

"A modern fable that resonates with echoes of timeless truths. The depth of the narrative is matched only by its enchanting charm."

- Porkington Ponderhooves, *Trotters & Tails Literary Quarterly*

"Witty, wise, and utterly captivating! This book stands as a testament to the enduring power of storytelling in our lives."

- Hamlet Swinelington, *Pigtropolis Herald*

"A piglet's journey from the depths to the heights, navigating shadows and discovering the whisper of unseen truths. A triumph of literary artistry!"

- Nibbletrotter Oinksworth, *Porker's Digest*

"In a world where pigs and wolves blur the lines, this story emerges as a clarion call to reclaim our identity. An unforgettable narrative that lingers in the mind."

 - Truffington McSquealers, III, *The Truffle Times*

"A rich blend of fantasy and reality, transporting readers into a world where piglets battle not just shadows but the complexities of their own hearts. A mesmerizing read!"

 - Percy Trottington, *New Sqweakland Review*

"With a stroke of genius, this tale unfolds, revealing profound insights beneath the whimsy. A delightful escapade into the heart of Pigletsville."

 - Penelope McSnout, *Swine Review Weekly*

"A literary gem that sparkles with wisdom and charm. An enchanting journey that leaves an indelible mark on the reader's soul."

 - Bristlebeard Pigleton, Jr., *Pen Sylvania Post*

"An epic saga that delves into the heart of Pigletsville, offering lessons that resonate far beyond the pages. A must-read for those seeking a timeless adventure."

 - Jambonette Swizzlehoof, *The Daily Slop*

"In this enchanting narrative, pigs and wolves come to life, dancing between the shadows and light. A tour de force of storytelling brilliance!"

 - Percival Hambleton, *Pigletshire Gazette*

"A beacon of literary brilliance, this story captivates with its profound messages, whimsical characters, and a narrative that echoes through the ages."

 - Muddyhoof Snufflepuff, *The Literary Trough Review*

"A most intolerant, hateful, deplorable cesspool of fictitious, fairytale rubbish! Illusory beliefs and pretentious slop prey upon unintelligent sensibilities of less evolved!"

 - Yellowfang Sizzleworthy, III, *The Wolven Syndicate*

THE MAGNIFICENT PIGLETS OF PIGLETSVILLE. © 2024 by Squigglesprout, Holland, Ohio. All rights reserved. Printed in the United States of America. For information, address Squigglesprout, Piglets@Squigglesprout.com.

www.squigglesprout.com

Names: Schlueter, Greg, 1967- author.
Title: The Magnificent Piglets of Pigletsville.
Description: First U.S. edition.
Holland, Ohio Squigglesprout, 2024.

Identifiers: ISBN 979-8-218-97273-8 (PB)
ISBN 979-8-218-97274-5 (eBook)
Cover art and design: *Willie of Pigletsville*
Created by Greg Schlueter
© Squigglesprout, Holland, Ohio 2024

Our books may be purchased in bulk. Please contact us by email at Piglets@Squigglesprout.com.

FORWARD

"The things I believed most then, the things I believe most now, are the things called fairy tales."
    - G.K. Chesterton

September, 2021. Lying in the intensive care unit, I could barely move. Or breathe. An oppressive omen lingered over me, painting the sterile walls in shades of death. I was in a void. Devoid of family or friends. Various beeps and mechanical sounds taunted me, discordant notes adding to an ever-growing cacophony orchestrated by some malevolent maestro waving his macabre baton over the planet. Wearing a crown. Pretending to be on the throne.

I became aware of the battle. And lived to tell about it.

This may be a fairytale, but don't make the mistake in thinking it is not real. It is very real. And consequential. In the shallows you will recognize present-day political personalities and circumstances; in the depths you will encounter our common aspiration for authentic belonging and becoming. Which happens on a battlefield. Involving formidable forces. Not simply for the likes of passing presidents, but transcending all ideologies. I invite you to go *there*.

"You were there. As was I. And I am now here. And will forever be."
    - Whisper of the Unseen

"In our pursuit of undermining piglet souls, we must consider the act of 'eating' them in a metaphorical sense. Just as piglets consume physical sustenance to sustain their bodies, we demons 'consume' their virtues and moral integrity to weaken their souls. We aim to devour their compassion, empathy, and goodness, replacing these qualities with selfishness, pride, and cruelty. The feasting we engage in is not one of nourishment but of corruption. As we dine upon their weaknesses and vices, we fatten ourselves on their descent into darkness."

    - Senior Aberrant Malphas to protégé, Grimner
      The Malphas Memos: Sizzilian Protocol

"Don't mistake redundancy for reverberation. One is splashing about in the shallows; the other, being drawn into the warm embrace of ever-greater depths."

    - Winston Hogsworth Willowbreeze

CONTENTS

DEDICATED TO OUR CHILDREN AND THEIR GENERATION OF WHOM IT WILL BE SAID: They were not deceived by the allure of Everywhere, and certainly, not Anywhere, but were drawn into a passionate pursuit of Somewhere. Guided by the whisper of Someone. In Whom they discovered and lived their magnificence.

And in doing so, changed the world.

PROLOGUE

The Enigmatic Mayor and His Sinister Strings

D eep in the heart of Pigletsville, a vibrant village cradled by rolling hills and lush pastures as green as emeralds, stood Willie, a wee piglet whose spirit surpassed his small frame. Willie was no ordinary porker; his tender years were marred by the sting of parental rejection as an orphan, a turbulent phase that paradoxically served as fertile ground later nurtured by the Bourby Gambit Guild. This peculiar yet distinguished assembly of elderly piglets was a camaraderie that matured through years spent playing chess and indulging in a modest sip of bourbon.

Before the present darkness came rolling in with the subtle malice of storm clouds, Willie's world revolved around his humble occupation as a newspaper boy. Seemingly insignificant, it placed him at the crossroads of Pigletsville's community. His diminutive stature became an unassuming advantage, a trusted magnet for the populace to confide their innermost thoughts and ideas. Willie observed the pulse of Pigletsville, standing apart from the usual sway of the town's affairs.

Unbeknownst to many, an unlikely mayor was shrouded in a secret as hazy as a smokehouse. Joe by name, wolf by nature, Mayor Joe Wolf was but a puppet, dangling by the strings of the enigmatic Deep Pen—a syndicate of wolves with a sinister agenda as black as a moonless night: advancing their bacon-making enterprise by infiltrating and dominating the village.

The wolves had mastered the art of deception, disguising themselves as piglets. Identifying as piglets. Wolves in piglets' clothing, you might say, as was Mayor Joe. He looked like a piglet in a very convincing costume, but underneath, his soul was as black as his true snout. The wolves were integrating into society with a malevolence punctuated by a certain ritual at their clandestine gatherings—the Wolven Conclaves.

There, at the Split Tree, we would find Draven Blackclaw, an ominous force of near preternatural genius, an incarnation of evil itself, with eyes that gleamed with the hunger of a blood moon and a sly grin eternally etched upon his snout. Blackclaw commanded his followers with chilling charisma and an ominous magnetism that twisted their allegiance to his will, spinning a web of fear and subservience with the precision of a master weaver.

The atmosphere charged with crackling electricity, Blackclaw would call his ravenous minions to order with a most vile proclamation: "If it looks like a piglet but *eats* a piglet..." All gathered would snarl uproariously, "It's a wolf!" Their collective howling would reverberate through the sinister assembly, an ear-piercing cacophony of raucous laughter and vigorous back-slapping.

Now, dear reader, you surely must be thinking, how could any creature be so wickedly disposed to regard our beloved piglets as little more than a mouth-watering, savory, crispy snack? Suspend your horror and disbelief for a moment. Woven within this grim narrative are profound lessons— lessons grave and consequential. Lessons that transcend Pigletsville's idyllic setting. If we curl a deaf ear now, we may one day find ourselves reduced to little more than sizzle in someone else's skillet!

PROLOGUE

Amid the ever-growing shadows, we will discover an undying spark in our beloved Willie, destined to ignite a flame beyond his meager capabilities. Enter Don Hairdo, commonly referred to as "The Do." He was a mysterious piglet with formidable political and cultural stature, afflicted with an extreme case of Narcissyndrome, which warped his character in ways both beneficial and beleaguering.

In a serendipitous connection between Willie and The Do, tragedy sets fire to dry parchment, breathing new life into the "deplorables" so branded by the sinister Wolven Syndicate. Hairdo galvanizes them with an unconventional yet steadfast determination to band together and fight back—a flicker of hope amidst the encroaching darkness.

This, dear friend, is the stage upon which we now stand with the magnificent piglets—engaged in an epic struggle. For those with eyes to see, we are participants in the eternal clash between forces of good and evil. If you dare to go there, to make this consequential odyssey, it is to the piglets' original magnificence we must turn.

INTRODUCTION
THE MAGNIFICENT PIGLETS

Like well-tuned fiddles playing a lively air in Pigletsville Square on any one of their many festival days, our beloved piglets were a harmonious blend of sharp minds, insatiable curiosity, and diligent ingenuity. But their true magic lay in the sweetness of their hearts and the goodness that flowed like a gentle stream through the fields of Pigletsville. Just as readily as the Taddy Torrent dispensed its riches to the parched earth, it would not be uncommon for any piglet at any time to set everything aside to welcome a stranger for a meal or a warm place to stay.

Renowned for their virtue, their lives were about progress, but not for its own sake. On the vast oceans of possibility, their rudders were not simply steered *Everywhere*, and certainly, not *Anywhere*, but *Somewhere*. *Somewhere* stood under a radiant Star guiding their purpose and illuminating a path otherwise shrouded in shadows.

But it was so much more. As *Somewhere* rose like majestic mountains above the barren plains of *Anywhere*, the piglets'

experience of pursuing *Somewhere* had the quality of a summons by a Someone. A supreme intelligence of surpassing splendor, definition, beauty, and majesty—with profound kindness and compassion—Who seemed to reach into their depths and breathe life into the same qualities.

This celestial Someone they referred to as the Whisper of the Unseen, or simply, the Whisper, was spoken of with unsurpassed reverence. The magnificence of our piglets lay precisely in their attunement to the Whisper, believed to endow them with mystical sensibilities, elevating them to celestial heights that illuminated their earthly path.

Accordingly, throughout history, often learning of *Somewhere* as much by rejection as by reception of the Whisper, they became more and more vigilant against Its principal adversary: Distraction, the subtle seducer on a relentless mission to lure its prey into the treacherous abyss, where the beast, Disordered Desire, waited.

CHAPTER 1
Till Depth Do We Part

In simple answer to an understandable inquiry, yes, in this magnificent land all are piglets. Regardless of age. A remarkable feature corresponding to their essence, exuding youthful exuberance throughout their years. Amidst the lively hustle and bustle of Pigletsville Square, piglets of all ages mingled and exchanged tidings of the day in an atmosphere that buzzed with vibrant energy. The air was filled with the sweet aroma of freshly baked acorn pies and the melodious chatter of piglets going about their daily routines.

At one corner of the Square, a group of piglets was gathered around a cart adorned with a vivid variety of fruits and vegetables. "Fresh carrots! Juicy apples!" cried the ever-cheerful Daisy Snoutworth, her rosy cheeks flushed with excitement as she enticed passersby with the bounty of her harvest.

In another corner, Wilhelmina Wigglesnout and Henrietta Hamhock, best of friends since their earliest days at Hoofington Hills Elementary, bustled about from store to store. Now, each with their own wee ones scampering alongside them, they wielded shopping bags and wrangled their energetic offspring while attempting to exchange complete sentences on tips and techniques for mud treatments.

Outside Trotters Tap House, a group of elderly piglets congregated, their laughter echoing amidst the vibrant chatter of the square. Clutching tankards of frothy ale, they exchanged tales of their youthful escapades, each story more embellished than the last.

At the fabulous Fatimore Fountain, just across from Swine and Grind Coffee Co., a pair of star-crossed young adult piglets shared a quaint table, their noses buried in steaming cups of Oinkaccino, exchanging shy smiles that spoke volumes.

And a most delightful expression of their exuberant culture, at Guadalahoofway Pavilion ("Hoofway") an impromptu dance party had broken out, with piglets of all ages twirling and spinning to the lively tunes of the famed fiddling duo, (Percival) Bowstrum & (Rufus) Fiddlestick. Hooves tapped in rhythm to the music, creating a joyful ruckus that lifted the spirits of all who passed by.

Dear reader, it is often said that a skilled storyteller doesn't simply tell a tale; instead, he paints vivid scenes that allow us to experience the intricacies of plot and character firsthand. While my primary aim is indeed to immerse you in these rich narratives, I find it necessary to illuminate certain profound truths nestled within the depths of our story. These truths, as tangible as the characters themselves, often dwell in the shadows, overlooked or obscured, yet they lie at the heart of the impending calamity we are soon to confront.

Among the cobblestone paths and thatched roofs that cradled dreams within their rustic embrace, the concept of "depth" in Pigletsville transcended mere abstraction. For our beloved piglets of Pigletsville, depth was in the rustling leaves of ancient trees, carrying secrets from eons past. Yet, it was also in the giggles and shared confidences under the sparkling moonlit sky, where hearts opened like blossoming petals.

Popularly speaking, depth was often regarded in the inter-piglet sense (between piglets) as something like a beach where some were watchers, quietly observing the world unfold like a tale in a storybook. Others were waders, taking gentle steps into deeper conversations but not venturing too far from the shore of the superficial. Then, there were the treaders, comfortably navigating the complexities of social interactions. Beyond them were the swimmers who dared to explore further, diving into deeper conversations and forging connections. Finally, there were the divers who sought the fathoms of genuine connection, which demands vulnerability and reveals the essence of one's soul.

In Pigletsville, these designations were not wielded as judgments. They were generally delivered with playful caprice, with a solemn understanding that no piglet could truly encapsulate another. For instance, at a lively gathering, one piglet might affectionately approach his solitary friend, "Ah, a watcher, I see!" Such a friend, slightly unnerved, might retort, "Indeed, a diver, I see!" Generally followed by something spirited, such as, "Didn't you see the 'no diving' sign?"

While depth was often bantered about playfully in conversations such as this, there is not one piglet among them who did not believe, did not profoundly revere, or genuinely pursue intra-piglet depth as a tenet; that is, an ultimate, relational reality within the soul. A meaningful anchoring and connection to a Someone. A very real Someone. Such was understood as the Whisper of the Unseen, entailing a kind of transcendence. A mystical but very real dance. In the truest sense, such are not just divers; they are Divers.

In the most accessible terms, as every piglet pines to be truly known by another as he desires to know another, because such is the currency of piglet existence, depth is an integral part of their story—a tale woven through the laughter that echoed in the village square and the whispered conversations in tiny back gardens. It was the essence that infused their every interaction, painting the world with vibrant hues of empathy, trust, and genuine friendship. Among the deeper divers, it is evident at any gathering where a luminary may command the enthusiasms of the masses for a moment, only to leave them afterward drowning in the shallows—having acquired only a phantom feeling of something dissipating as swiftly as a breeze.

It's the uncelebrated divers who constitute the heart. They are the unseen suns illuminating the soul of piglet existence, around whom all gravitate without even realizing it. Their egos have been purged of superficial aspirations. They don't care about being "in," as it is merely a dressed-up way of being without. They don't care about getting ahead, as it tends to mean leaving *Somewhere* behind. Fellow piglets trust them and go to them because they don't leave you wondering what they will do with your entrustment. Divers exude quiet confidence because wherever they are is precisely where they mean to be. That makes them a safe harbor—a treasure beyond compare.

It must be noted that such value was acquired at a great cost, forged through tumultuous seasons of risk, trust, and vulnerability. And a whole lot of trust broken over time. Repeatedly.

And so it was, amid the joyful chaos of the public square, that our unsuspecting hero, Willie, stood with a stack of newspapers tucked under his arm, his keen eyes observing the scene with a mixture of amusement and affection. As he made his way through the crowd, he exchanged cheerful greetings and friendly banter with his fellow piglets, his warm smile spreading infectious joy wherever he went.

In the forthcoming chapter, we will delve deeper into Willie's life. As an orphaned runt, shuffled from one household to another, always yearning for the warmth of a true home, his story punctuates that if one does not allow the inevitable splintering of trust to crush his belief in depth, if he can resist erecting an impenetrable fortress to protect himself from the inevitable hurt, if he perseveres, he will find himself forged in wisdom, bequeathed a quality beyond compare.

CHAPTER 2
The Bourby Gambit Guild

Willie wore a faded vest, patched at the edges, and trousers that seemed a tad too short. But it was the weathered, jaunty newsboy cap perched slightly askew atop his head that had become his signature. In such unassuming attire, he was a sight to behold. Much like his demeanor, such donning seemed to embrace the stories of the past, woven into each stitch and fray. His snout, often adorned with a tiny, contented smile, was like a beacon of warmth in the cool breezes of their storied land.

Willie moved with a certain gait— every few steps marked by a distinctive little skip, a sort of dance revealing inner delight. Such peculiarities were not off-putting; they were his trademarks, endearing him to the piglets of Pigletsville. There was even the proverbial twinkle in his eyes that sparkled with wisdom beyond his years.

Willie's interests were simple yet profound. Outside his most cherished moments basking in the glow of the Bourby Gambit Guild, whom we shall meet shortly, he found solace in the pages of old books, their weathered covers and musty scent inviting him into realms of forgotten tales. His fascination with the world around him was evident in how he'd pause to observe a lone wildflower growing amid the cobblestones, finding beauty in the most overlooked places.

In the shallows, before the greater public, our beloved Willie was generally dismissed as mundane; he had no aspirations that caught the eye or dreams that reached for the stars. His joy lay not in achieving but in merely existing—a steadfast mooring in the storms of life. He cared little for keeping up with the whirlwinds others chased; he was content being himself. Thus, when the winds of change howled, as we shall soon discover, Willie stood unaffected, his ego sheltered on the sidelines, indifferent to impressing others.

But it was in Willie's closest interactions that he truly shone. Despite being a runt, his size never diminished the enormity of his heart. Not unlike the seeds of a once-hidden Squigglesprout unfolding with the caress of sunlight, so Willie's character began to unfold in the illumination of the enigmatic Bourby Gambit Guild, whom he encountered years earlier.

Before getting to this truly momentous turn in his life, a word on Squigglesprout, the most enchanting floral wonder in all the world. In proportion to the sunlight bathing its delicate form, the mystical blue Squigglesprout hums a melodic tune which, amid its august company on a radiant summer day, becomes a chorus reverberating through the air. Each of its leaflets seems to sway in rhythm, adding a whimsical ballet to the garden's ensemble. Its sprightly nature draws others near, inviting them to partake in its infectious mirth.

Now, if we were to regard a select gathering in Pigletsville as the embodiment of the most exquisite bourbon, meticulously blended from the rarest elements, refined through age and experience, it would surely be the Bourby Gambit Guild, or as they are more commonly regarded, the Bourbies. This cadre of seasoned piglets shared a bond woven of chess and the shared indulgence of a wee nip of bourbon. Yes, bourbon. With its golden hues akin to a honeybee's dance in the late summer sun, that ambient elixir held a charm that could coax laughter from even the grumpiest old oak tree in the woods. Its aroma, a concerto of caramel and oak, whispered tales of forgotten journeys across distant lands. Sipping it was like embracing an old friend, a delightful dance between warmth and mischief that tickled the senses and sparked stories untold.

Forgive me for getting carried away with such reverie about Squigglesprout, bourbon, and all the rest. Such, again, is the magnificent nature of Pigletsgville culture. A profound appreciation for the smallest things. I see them as ornate threads that comprise a rich tapestry binding them all together.

Let's return to the day that set this fortuitous association in motion.

After completing his paperboy duties, Willie would pass a small corner of Pigletsville Square where, just outside Trotters Tap House, the Bourby Gambit Guild would be engrossed for hours over what appeared to him as no more than arbitrarily moving odd statuary. Without ever having the courage to cross over the invisible boundaries marking their hallowed ground, Willie watched them, and as he grew older, he began to experience something like a summons.

It wasn't the lure of chess, a game he scarcely comprehended, nor the allure of bourbon, which held the mystique of fire in a bottle. No, amidst the shards of loneliness and adversity, it was the hearty laughter. It was a harmony of souls, an orchestration of mirth that reached beyond. The chuckles and guffaws became an intangible overture that played chords of delight in the souls of all passersby, chords that resonated within him. It was what he only later came to understand as friendship.

It was as if his life had been a sort of scale; one side dug into the muddied earth under the weight of his splintered soul.

Laden with doubts, fears, and insecurities. Lost in the abyss of *Anywhere*. But with each moment spent in the presence of the Bourbies, he felt Something within himself. A constant weight of grappling giving way. And then, one day, it happened. An ever-growing summons within him culminated with enough Something to overwhelm his reserve. Unseen hooves seemed to reach out and gently but firmly draw Willie to the bench under the Twinkleleaf Ash—all but seven steps from Bourby territory.

Through ordinary eyes, all you would have seen is an ordinary piglet making his ordinary way towards an ordinary bench. But for Willie, in his depths, each step was an extraordinary reach. With each step, he was discovering a window in his soul he didn't know existed, through which he experienced an invigorating breeze the likes of which he had never known. An encounter of Something lifting him above all that had him buried. With each step, Willie was exchanging *Anywhere* for the exhilaration of *Somewhere*. In this, Willie was becoming aware of a summons by a Someone. To become part of Something. With each step, Willie was discovering he was someone.

And so, following that day, he found himself filled with just enough Something to return the next day. And the day after that. The ever-opening window became a door.

No more than a week later, Milfred Snoutsworth, proudly rotund and ever-choking-on-a-cigar, coughed through mud-talking to his sullen opponent, Barnaby Trottersby, who was staring catatonically at the board. "Now, Barns! Nae amount of starin' at yer dead royalty is gonna raise 'em from the grave!" Laughter amid coughing. "Why dinnae ye consult the wee lad o'er there? He's in a grander spot than ye!"

All broke into warm laughter that others might find excessive, not understanding that such was the elemental language among these jovial friends who simply loved to laugh. Embarrassment painted Willie's cheeks flush red. Perched on his seat, his legs swung back and forth like the pendulum of a grandfather clock. He observed a distinguished figure among them, a piglet of venerable bearing, tapping his pipe and rising deliberately, as if embracing the passage of time, to make his way toward Willie.

Despite being a runt, his size never diminished the enormity of his heart. Not unlike the seeds of a once-hidden Squigglesprout unfolding with the caress of sunlight, so Willie's character began to unfold in the illumination of the enigmatic Bourby Gambit Guild, whom he encountered years earlier.

CHAPTER 3
PAWN OF GREAT PRICE

In his grandfatherly way, McPorcinski addressed Willie with a warmth that wrapped around the lad's reluctance. "Ye needn't stay lurkin' in the shadows, laddie! Every table yearns for camaraderie; just over there, a seat seems to beckon yer name!"

Willie hesitated, with doubts still weighing heavily on his shoulders. Not unlike his first grand steps to the bench, buoyed by an exhilaration of navigating through the murky clouds of *Anywhere* into the sunlit horizon of *Somewhere*, these steps toward the table seemed to stretch across an eternity, each stride marked with uncertainty yet laced with determination. Corresponding to the ever-greater exchange of Anything for Something. Finally crossing into their inner circle, his heart pounded a tune of eagerness and apprehension.

Across from McPorcinski, Willie gingerly took the seat offered, slowly settling into it as if it were an extension of his being. The chair felt familiar, as though it had long awaited his arrival. With each passing moment in its embrace, Willie's once-reluctant spirit found solace, a sense of belonging blooming within him. It was as though this very spot had anticipated his presence.

Before Willie knew it, he found before him liquid amber cascading into a waiting glass. McPorcinski's gesture toward the peculiar statuary was simple yet laden with meaning. "Welcome... a-board," he intoned softly as a unified chorus of clinking glasses and hearty cheers filled the air. "Hear, hear!"

Ever since that first burning sip passed his lips, setting his small frame afire, a periodic, wee spot of bourbon came to mean so much. A cherished bond among piglets that grew much richer through the years. One of mutual delight, admiration, and affection. A solitary piglet much the younger, with them, he felt himself king of the world. More privileged than anyone he could imagine.

Along with the bourbon, chess embodied something deeper for these wonderfully weathered sages. Something ultimate. Life's grand pursuit of wisdom. Chess reveals reality to be something we can't so much break, only be broken against. Along with the physical and moral universe, chess has sure guidelines. Decisions better or worse. Black and white, you might say. Entailing feelings and emotions, certainly! But not under their tyranny. Based upon reality we cannot so much determine, but in which we are determined.

In the tapestry of their existence, profound meanings didn't just adorn their play; they intricately wove themselves into the very fabric of their existence. From the enchanting melodies echoing through their music, to the strokes of brilliance on canvases, and the verses dancing off parchments, every element resonated with depth. It was an immersion, an embrace that never waned. And all this punctuated by the perennial emergence of the resplendent Maiden Falls, where the exuberant Theodorus Torrent, affectionately known as the Taddy Torrent, flowed gracefully through the heart of Pigletsville. These waters weren't mere streams; they were enduring symbols, epitomizing the essence of their cherished piglets. As the revered sage,

Winston H. Willowbreeze once remarked: "Here's tae the chess, the unyielding bastion that guides the course of truth, like the banks of the river! And here's tae the bourbon, swirling like the lively waters of the Taddy!"

For Willie, having grown up feeling little more than an inconsequential runt, he related to the pawns— so diminutive and powerless. Initially, all those years ago, he regarded pawns as little more than an accessory. They were in the way, just something meant to be sacrificed. He related to all that. But under the grandfatherly kindness of McPorcinski, Willie came to understand the inestimable value of each pawn. And himself. Particularly when they worked together.

Pawns are formidable precisely because they are small, meek, and humble. Accordingly, they are underestimated. A value hidden. Yet, in the right place and at the right time, one pawn can completely shift the game. In fact, unlike all the other pieces, only the pawn has the hidden capacity to be transformed into something much greater.

With each passing day, Willie was awakening more and more to an awareness that he was beloved because of who he was. Something like a pawn. He was coming to understand a pawn's supreme nobility in making a strategic sacrifice. For something greater. For the king. To win the game. And these chess-playing noble piglets affectionately welcomed him in their courts.

CHAPTER 4
Inconspicuous Sage in Public Square

Amid the bustling streets and lively corners of Pigletsville's public square, where piglets mingled and exchanged tidings of the day, Willie stood—small in stature but a formidable confidant for those who pined for depth.

This square was more than just a marketplace for papers; it was a theater of opinion where the weight of news collided with the gravity of individual perspectives. Here, opinions were forged and swayed, chiseled by the tales the newspapers spun and the interactions they sparked.

Let us listen in on a typical exchange that took place one brisk morning in Pigletsville. As the sun painted golden hues across the cobblestone streets, Mr. Eleazor Snodberry, a distinguished piglet adorned in a finely tailored waistcoat, approached Willie's newsstand with an air of both regality and curiosity. The rustling papers whispered their headlines, enticing the patrons with information.

"Good morning, young Willie," Mr. Snodberry greeted with

 15

a tip of his snout. "What intriguing tales unfold in the press today?"

Willie, acknowledging the esteemed president of the Hamington Bank, took his part in the morning ritual. With a respectful nod while exchanging a pristine paper for payment, including a wee bit more than required, Willie returned the sentiments first imparted the very first time they'd met years ago. "Good morning, Mr. Snodberry. All the news unfit to be printed awaits!"

Mr. Snodberry's eyes twinkled with a combination of wisdom and mischief as he replied, "Thank you, my dear boy." With the paper in his hooves, Mr. Snodberry took his usual place by the newsstand. Opening the crisp pages, he perused the headlines and then turned his gaze toward Willie. "What do you make of Old Joe's new policy on Pigletsville's borders? Quite the strategic move, wouldn't you say?"

Willie, ever thoughtful, offered a reply veiled in reflection. "Borders, Mr. Snodberry, are like the edges of a masterpiece. What is a picture without lines?"

A gleam of approval flashed in Mr. Snodberry's eyes. "Ah, an artist's perspective, I see. And what of this hogwash about wolves infiltrating Pigletsville? Any credence to such claims?"

Willie, choosing his words with measured care, responded, "Wolves, like shadows, are often whispered about. But consider, sir, what defines a shadow? Is it not merely an absence of light?"

Mr. Snodberry chuckled, appreciating the philosophical dance. "Indeed, young Willie, your insights are as enlightening as ever. Now, about the Pigsty's chances in the playoffs—any predictions?"

Willie, with a playful glint in his eye, pondered, "Playoffs, Mr. Snodberry, are the culmination of effort, where the game transcends the players. Do you believe fate is written or forged on the field?"

Their daily dialogue continued, a dance of questions and reflections, as Willie navigated the intricate choreography of thought with the esteemed president. In those moments, the newsstand transformed into a stage where wisdom and curiosity waltzed together, leaving both piglets enriched by the exchange.

It was in conversations such as this and so many others that Willie, the unlikely sage, would scratch his little piglet head in bewilderment at the penchant for so many to stir up such complexities from such simple truths. How a splintered ego would unnecessarily warp and inflate something as plain as the snout on one's face.

As a paperboy, while others sought validation through alignment with popular opinions, Willie remained immune, not seeking to fit in, for his wisdom lay not in capricious conformity, but in the simple, straightforward, self-evident, *smallness* of truth. Such smallness wasn't small-mindedness; it was a gift—a vantage point from which he saw beyond the superficial, beyond the frenzy of opinion-making. He was a beacon of clarity and truth in a storm of swirling thoughts and false narratives.

Before us, dear reader, is the primordial question of character and its capacity to solidly anchor one amid a whirlwind of ever-shifting perspectives and clamorous narratives. Even more, the capacity to influence. In Willie's presence, others discovered a humble tranquility that inspired them to think. This was a matter of great consequence, with far-ranging effects which we shall soon see.

CHAPTER 5
THE BALLAD OF SAGELIA

N ow, dear reader, join me as we dive more deeply into the depths that define our beloved piglets as we behold a truly enchanting myth passed down through their generations. A tale darker than the shadows cast by the ancient trees that embraced their village. Yet, this desolation beckoned the unfettered souls among them to anticipate the radiant light that would soon rise, banishing shadows with each passing moment. This light would bathe their world in a brilliance that mirrored their nature, magnificent and enduring.

The cherished epic, known as the *Ballad of Sagelia*, is an enchanting saga of unwavering valor and selflessness. It remains etched into the collective memory of Pigletsville, transcending generations with its timeless message. It unfolds something like this.

In the vibrant heart of Pigletsville lived a young piglet known as Sagelia, whose grace and boundless compassion set her apart from her peers. Unlike other piglets, Sagelia possessed a unique gift—a keen insight into the elusive nature of Distraction, the cunning force that could ensnare her fellow piglets and lead them astray into the clutches of Disordered Desire. With a gaze that pierced through veils of deception, Sagelia could discern the subtle whispers of temptation, redirecting wayward souls back towards the path of purpose. For when the lures of *Everywhere* and *Anywhere* threatened to eclipse the beacon of *Somewhere*, it was Sagelia who stood as a steadfast guardian, protecting the delicate harmony of inter-piglet joy and fulfillment.

Now, the village had long thrived on the strength of their unity and selfless regard for one another. They shared their labor, laughter, hopes, and dreams, bound by the core virtues of their community. Dignity, purpose, invention, diligence, and kindness were the lifeblood of Pigletsville, and under the protective canopy of the Whisper, they had flourished.

However, a foreboding shadow crept over Pigletsville, an omen that threatened the very foundations of their joyful existence.

In the heart of Pigletsville, a nefarious creature named Divertusis slithered into their blissful world, a stranger cloaked in the disguise of a piglet. The piglets had no inkling of the malevolence that lurked beneath his luminous facade.

Divertusis was an enigma, appearing to them so radiant and so gentle that the pure-hearted piglets were easily swayed by his pretentious acts of concern and kindness. The village, known for its boundless goodwill, could not see through his masquerade.

The creature, a master of deceit, began his subtle campaign, sowing seeds of disinterest, selfishness, and entitlement among the unsuspecting piglets. As unity began to fray and contention replaced harmony, the once-cordial relations of Pigletsville started to crumble.

Only Sagelia, with her keen senses, saw through the charade. Under a brooding evening sky, illuminated by the radiant gleam of a full moon, Sagelia stealthily followed Divertusis to a hidden lair, where, concealed from his sight, she witnessed his true form—a grotesque, hideous brute. Divertusis stood before Shadowglass, a mystical mirror framed by broken bones, whispering to a shadowy, malevolent figure known as the Lord of Shadows. It became clear that Divertusis was but an evil emissary in a sinister game.

The Lord of Shadows had an insidious plan—a plan to turn the hearts of the piglets without ever revealing his existence. Suddenly, he sensed Sagelia's presence, realizing that she held the knowledge that could thwart their evil plot. He threatened to harm her family if she dared to reveal Divertusis's true identity.

Reluctantly, on the promise that her beloved family would not be harmed by their nefarious play, Sagelia agreed to a malevolent pact. With a drop of her blood, the Lord of Shadows bound her life to his own, a connection that could only be severed by shattering Shadowglass.

As time passed, the enchantment of Divertusis deepened its hold on Pigletsville. One by one, he was gaining control. The piglets were no longer paragons of kindness and unity. Instead, they were succumbing to selfishness, entitlement, and even malice. Sagelia keenly observed the repercussions, especially the impact on her cherished little brother, Jubilano, whose innate goodness faced the looming threat of consumption by the pernicious predator. Inevitably, she found herself in a relentless tug-of-war with Divertusis, each vying for control over the very soul of her beloved sibling.

When things came to a fevered pitch, on a fateful night when storm clouds marred the light of a blood moon, with even her own family teetering on the brink of succumbing to the Lord of the Shadows, Sagelia undertook her perilous journey to the hidden lair. Armed with her family's ancestral staff, she shattered the mirror, which ended the Lord of Shadows' reign of darkness.

And her own life.

The evil lord's demise revealed Divertusis's true form and the enchantment lifted from the piglets. Unity and kindness returned to Pigletsville, and their moral compass pointed Due North once more. Sagelia's act of self-sacrificing bravery had freed them from the clutches of Divertusis and the Lord of Shadows.

This tale underscored the timeless truth that Pigletsville held dear. So long as they remained attuned to the Whisper, illumination of the path to *Somewhere* would vanquish even the darkest shadows spun by the lords of *Anywhere*. The lessons learned from Sagelia's heroic sacrifice were etched into their hearts and minds.

Throughout Pigletsville on any given day, throughout their noble land, you'd hear them sing this ancient hymn:

'NEATH NOBLE SKIES AND SHADOWS' PLIGHT,
IN PIGLETSVILLE'S SERENE MOONLIGHT.
SAGELIA, BLESSED, WITH EYES TO SEE,
FELT DISTRACTION'S DEADLY ENMITY.
DIVERTUSIS, IN GUILE ARRAYED,
WOVE DISCORD WITH A MASQUERADE.
'NEATH THE FULL MOON'S WATCHFUL GAZE,
SAGELIA UNVEILED HIS WICKED WAYS.
A PACT IN SHADOWS, FORGED WITH CARE,
TO SHIELD HER KIN FROM SHADOWS' SNARE.
WITH ANCESTRAL STAFF, THROUGH DARKNESS TROD,
SHATTERING ILLUSIONS, BREAKING THE FLAWED.
PIGLETSVILLE, ONCE VEILED IN NIGHT,
BY SAGELIA'S SACRIFICE, EMERGED IN LIGHT.
GUIDED BY THE WHISPER'S LORE,
MAGNIFICENT FOREVERMORE.

So, you surely now must wonder, given such resplendent qualities of our beloved piglets anchored so deeply in such a magnificent myth, how did ravenous wolves sway much of the piglet populace toward their sinister goals? We must return to where our story continues to unfold—the emergence and establishment of Deep Pen, ancient masters of cunning, birthed in the mysterious, malevolent realm of Animas Aberratas.

CHAPTER 6
The Malphas Memos: Sizzilian Protocol

P icking up where we left off in Pigletsville, we are drawn to the serene beauty of the hamlet, nestled amidst rolling hills and verdant pastures nourished by the invigorating flow of the Taddy Torrent. In this tranquil setting resides Willie, a humble orphan whose spirit transcends his modest stature, nurtured within the warm camaraderie of the Bourby Gambit Guild. Our dear piglets, akin to flickering sparks dancing around a crackling campfire on a crisp autumn eve, are entwined in tales brimming with vitality, each echoing a spirited pursuit of *Somewhere* guided by an elusive Someone, steeped in the quest for genuine depth—all cocooned within the tender embrace of an unseen Whisper. This harmonious symphony resonates at the heart of the hamlet's revered legend, the enchanting *Ballad of Sagelia.*

Now, enter Deep Pen, a shadowy syndicate of sinister influencers ("The Syndicate") lurking in the depths of Pigletsville. Though they wield power, they themselves are under a baton of ancient masters of cunning, forged in the noxious fumes of

Animas Aberratas—the darkest realm of preternatural power. Their very essence is the absence of that which is good, true and beautiful, which is to say, they are at war with the Whisper of the Unseen.

How, you surely must ask, did magnificent piglets endowed with so much good find themselves in such an oppressed condition? That is the question of the moment. And here it shall be answered.

Only toward the end of this tumult did revolutionary piglets (whom we shall soon meet) come upon a truly chilling collection of memo fragments somehow acquired from Animas Aberratus, only some of which were translated. These were discovered in the highly secretive Trotter Trove of the late preeminent scholar, Winston Hogsworth Willowbreeze, following his very untimely and suspicious death. (A remarkable story in itself to be sure, but it must await another telling.)

Under the title, "Into the Skillet: Strategies for Sizzling Swine," or commonly referred to as the Sizzilian Protocol, the translated fragments chronicle a truly ominous exchange between a Senior Aberrant named Malphas and Grimner, his protégé, leader of Sinister Cultivators of Unfathomable Misery (S.C.U.M.). Within these fragments lies a window into the machinations of Animas Aberratas—a calculated orchestration of malevolence born from thorough examination of the piglets' motivations, weaknesses, and inclinations. This meticulous undertaking aimed to seduce them into embracing Aberrant dominion.

The Sizzilian Protocol paved the way for the establishment of Deep Pen, Animas Aberratus' physical enclave of wolves among the piglets of Pigletsville. This insidious underground organization included many piglets they succeeded in corrupting.

Let us now turn to the notable fragments from Willowbreeze's collection.

MEMO 1: Sizzilian Protocol (Into the Skillet: Strategies for Sizzling Swine)

Objective: The Broad Stroke
To: Grimner, Vice Aberrant, S.C.U.M.
From: Malphas, Senior Aberrant

In our pursuit of undermining piglet souls, we must consider the act of 'eating' them in a metaphorical sense. Just as piglets consume physical sustenance to sustain their bodies, we demons 'consume' their virtues and moral integrity to weaken their souls. We aim to devour their compassion, empathy, and goodness, replacing these qualities with selfishness, pride, and cruelty. The feasting we engage in is not one of nourishment but of corruption. As we dine upon their weaknesses and vices, we fatten ourselves on their descent into darkness.

These memos concern a critically important matter—the final phase of our war against our Enemy by way of seducing and devouring It's beloved swine! My loathsome Grimner, the most despicable glory awaits us on the other side of this Sizzilian Protocol. Herein lies our stratagem, our intricate orchestration of total dominion over Pigletsville. We know our menu for our feast; it's time to set the table! Through our deputy, Draven Blackclaw, and the greater establishment of Deep Pen, we shall conduct a symphony of perversion, each dissonant note a tantalizing turn, enabling us to seduce piglet depths. Behold our infernal score, piece by nefarious piece!

In our most rotten core, we are about one thing: Seduction. Our diabolical work can never be so brazen, monumental, or all at once lest it shocks their sensitive attunement to our Enemy. No, our work must be gradual. While at the outset, this will involve the most pleasing tyranny, such is only to confuse and dishearten so that we can cultivate their abject hatred of all authority! Particularly that of our Enemy! How much more formidable it will be to gain their willful cooperation, their willful exchange of *Somewhere* for *Anywhere*! In this macabre dance, we will impel them to surrender [vulgar term for Someone] for Anyone, which is to say, us! Sizzle!

Thus, the meaning of the motto that adorns our headquarters of S.C.U.M.: "Minuscule steps forward, eternal separation!" Each small indulgence, each minute deviation, is a delicious morsel leading them further from the light. All hail our Master who has so splendidly decreed this Protocol!

Certainly, this elaborate scheme hinges upon the establishment of Deep Pen. Through its gradual infiltration and corruption, sacred boundaries once unquestioned by individual piglets will become curiosities. Curiosities will become options; options will transform into offerings; offerings will evolve into commonplace; and the commonplace will evolve into institutional obligation, encroaching upon every aspect of piglet life!

Sizzilism, our economic masterpiece, will fuel the inferno! We will offer trinkets and Hogbacks to forge entitlement, which they will readily accept in exchange for their empowerment. In this, they will become dependent, their spark extinguished, making them ripe for the picking!

But fear, Grimner, fear is the maestro's most exquisite instrument! The Wuham Virus, our maleficent masterpiece of Aberratus Engineering, will sow terror, paving the way for Sqweak Sauce, the nectar of our control. And all of this legitimized through our control of their media, particularly the Piglet Nirvana Network (PNN) and the *New Pork Times*, which will amplify the fear and confusion while we, the unseen puppeteers, tighten the strings! Hear the sizzle!

MEMO 2: Sizzilian Protocol (Into the Skillet: Strategies for Sizzling Swine)

Objective: Descent Into Desolation
To: Grimner, Vice Aberrant, S.C.U.M.
From: Malphas, Senior Aberrant

In your recent reply, you petulantly pointed out that I have only sketched the broad strokes! Patience is the artist's virtue, my friend! (Even we aberrants require some!) Every masterpiece commences with the careful crafting of its background. With the darkness of Master's soul now laid bare upon the canvas, we may proceed to the intricate layers that follow.

At the very outset, we will exploit the shallows. See those swine, flitting about, more concerned with the whispers of their peers than the Whisper of truth? More afraid of standing out than standing firm? These are our fodder! We will play our discordant notes, not as a blaring fanfare, but as a seductive undercurrent, a melody of conformity, acceptance, and hogwash so pervasive, so intoxicating, that the piglets will dance themselves into our sumptuous spread! Sizzle!

Our next act of malice will be to shatter the very mirror

 26

of truth, Objectivity. Envision a world where "wolf" could just as readily denote "piglet" and "bacon" hailed as "betterment"! A tantalizing chaos, would you not concur? Ah, the aroma of sizzling bacon! In this distorted realm, we sow the seeds of Feeling, not as mere emotions but as infallible, unquestioned, monstrous idols. Enter our despised comrade, Disordered Desire! Empowering us to enthrone their emotions with barbed wire and deceit, each whim a twisted compass guiding them deeper into our snare.

Next, with Objectivity obliterated and Feeling at the helm, our pathetic little piglets will presume themselves to be under their own power. Magnificent piglets, ha! What a magnificent delusion! It is then we will weave a tapestry of our meanings into the likes of "privacy," "tolerance," and even "love," each thread a lie spun with venomous delight.

What grand amusement it shall be to witness these pitiful creatures waving banners of "tolerance" with such sanctimonious fervor, selectively applying it to that which is *ours*, bad and false, while remaining *intolerant* of that which is good and true! Oblivious to the truth that if words can mean anything, they lose all meaning. And in that void, everything becomes ours to manipulate and control. Oh, the savory sizzle of our impending dominion!

My grotesque Grimner, throughout history, we have masqueraded as Pied Pipers! Let them never have the slightest indication that we are, in fact, Maleficent Maestros, weaving discordant notes in seductive movements that lead the piglets on a merry dance to their demise.

We will hide behind inane, dismissive pronouncements sewn in their pathetic piglet souls, such as "your truth" and "who are you to say," as if the entire landscape of existence is a plaything of their passion! "Who dares to judge?" we'll hiss, silencing dissent with the chilling comfort of ambiguity. (Let them never know that Objectivity is something we ourselves are beholden to!)

MEMO 3: Sizzilian Protocol (Into the Skillet: Strategies for Sizzling Swine)

Objective: Casting Hurls Before Swine
To: Grimner, Vice Aberrant, S.C.U.M.
From: Malphas, Senior Aberrant

You must indulge me for my ingenious title! "Hurls Before Swine"! Ha! I do hope you are having a good belly laugh! If not, well, sanctify you!

We are so cursed (thank Aberration!) to see and desire the worst of these creatures. Not as they are, but as we are! In a preternatural sense, we "consume" that despicable image, letting it marinate and churn in the foul, putrid bowls of our noxious bellies, and then regurgitate it to them as a palatable feast appealing to their warped appetites.

Now more directly, how, you ask, do we deal with their ever-growing ache of absence along the way? That visceral reminder bequeathed them by our Adversary of a wayward rudder? You inane peon! By now you ought to know we are Maleficent Maestros! Titans of Twist! The better question: How do we orchestrate their dissonance so they choose to be more distant? So they become all the more contemptuous, and their souls, more cavernous?

Why, my pernicious pupil, at every step along the perilous path of seduction we will anesthetize them with just the right whisper! Just the right amount of distraction! For instance, as those insufferable notes of the *Ballad* may spark, reaching up from sacred depths we have yet to tarnish, we douse them with dismissal: "Don't be silly! It's a phantom memory! A fleeting sentiment! A thing of fairytales! Something thoroughly unreliable!" This is best followed up by ingratiating their egos, "You're much more clever!"

How spectacularly amusing it will be to see them invoke the very thing we've gotten them to disregard, Objectivity, while, in fact, they act under our dominion of Feeling!

At the very core, in their deepest depths, it's about identity. A formidable foe we can not fight in its essence, as they are fashioned of [vulgar term for Someone]! It is their indomitable nature. Thus, amid their inner maelstrom of deceit and lies, where we paint *their* identities according to *our* desires, we must keep whispering, "*This* is what is! *This* is you!" When they come to accept our version, when they come to accept that shapeless, aimless squish as *their identity*, we'll know we have full access to their thrones! What a grand play it will be! Cloaked in clouds of self-satisfaction, they will be dancing on our strings.

Yes, while for some inexplicable reason, the Whisper will be ever in pursuit of intra-piglet depth with each one, no matter how far they've strayed, such confers upon them the capacity to choose or reject. As our petulant little swine increasingly find themselves held fast by the shackles of their own rejection, their pleas lost in the echoes of their own self-imposed dungeons—as such pleas are uttered seemingly without answer, they will first presume the Whisper indifferent. Having turned their gaze inward, making themselves the focal point of their own existence, they will fail to grasp that they desire an impossibility: the Whisper to bend to *their* wills!

As they struggle to cast off the remnants of shame, they will inevitably don the jagged cloaks of contempt—directed towards the Whisper, the *Ballad*, and all who hold them in regard. And so on. Whether our Enemy exists will be of no consequence. Our work will have been accomplished. They will cease to care.

And of our feast? Fret not, my maleficent maestro! In such insidious subjugation they will be subdued but not silent! We will not be deprived of their shrieks! With the Enemy evicted, we will have front-row seats to a grand symphony of unspoken cries from desolate depths, consumed by dissonance they've been formed to dismiss, a crescendo for our delectable amusement!

Are you ready for the sizzle?

Needless to say, dear reader, these Malphas Memos were executed with meticulous, pernicious precision. Over many seasons, much of our beloved piglet populace was seduced, willfully coming under the diabolical subjugation of Deep Pen. Which is to say, under the tyranny of the diabolical Animas Aberratas. As their faculties dulled and the *Ballad of Sagelia* faded from their souls, they succumbed to a state of numbness and vulnerability. Worse, in their splintered state, a kind of self-contempt and animosity was projected upon any who resisted such evil.

Amid the encroaching malevolence, Willie and the Bourbies emerged, anchored in unseen depths, resilient in pursuit of truth, and unwavering in allegiance to the sweet melody of the *Ballad*. It is to them that our tale now turns.

CHAPTER 7
BATTLE AGAINST DARKNESS

T he heart of Pigletsville was under siege. As Willie assumed his paperboy perch in the center of town, the atmosphere around him grew dense with an unspoken malignancy. Fellow piglets, once eager for his friendship and his quiet wisdom, now seemed distant. They no longer sought his anchoring presence; they were adrift in the sea of misinformation. They were buying into the falsities strewn across the Deep Pen-controlled papers, believing every word that twisted reality into an incomprehensible knot.

What's most tragic is that the vibrant culture of many magnificent piglets in pursuit of *Somewhere* was slowly devolving. Instead of pursuing *Everywhere* or *Anywhere*, which at least entailed interest and purpose, our beloved piglets were falling into an abyss never before considered: a sedated state of numbed indifference known as *Nowhere*.

Without the spark of purpose, many were just plain giving up. The buoyant winds that once billowed their sails were abruptly vanishing, leaving them adrift on a boundless sea of insignificance. For Willie, who harbored a resilient spirit despite these desolate tides, a quiet but poignant sadness etched itself into his gaze. He beheld the heart-wrenching sight of his companions slowly fading into the labyrinthine haze of deceit, their once-gleaming spirits dulled by the shadows of a hollow existence.

More ominous, some piglets, once vibrant and full of life, disappeared without a trace, rumors whispering that they had met a terrible fate, transformed into the very thing that often ended up on a Deep Pen breakfast plate.

One day, as he was on his routine walk home, so eager for chess, a wee nip of bourbon, and yes, above all, the companionship that had so come to fill his life, he was horrified to find that hallowed ground outside Trotters Tap House completely vacant. A vacancy that reverberated in his soul.

A frenzied torrent of dread seized him with unrelenting claws. Were his cherished companions whisked away? Did they disappear into hiding? An unnerving thought, like a specter, lingered at the precipice of his consciousness, seeking to take root in his mind. Yet, Willie, resolute, pushed it away with the strength of a defiant gust, refusing to yield to its chilling implications.

Only after a long moment staggering under the oppressive weight of concern for his friends did he consider himself. Was The Syndicate after *him*? Was *he* being watched? After all, he was a Bourby. Whatever fate befell them hung over him like a menacing cloud.

Right then, he understood the deeper truth of words frequently uttered by Milfred Snoutsworth, typically while announcing he's taking his opponent's Queen: "We dinnae grasp the gem until she's vanished." Gone was the comfortable ease with which he used to traverse the serene and safe village. Without fear. Without suspicion. Never thinking it could be otherwise. Gone was the spark of life. Glancing around, he was struck by the sea of downcast faces. Consumed in their clouds. Isolated from one another. How had such a fate befallen such magnificent piglets?

Not unlike others who only experience real tragedy from such a distance, safely wrapped in the security and comfort of their cozy chairs, regarding it as the sort of thing that only happens to others (and therefore, finding it so easy to dismiss it all by simply turning the page), every day, more and more, Willie was finding himself and his community in the story. And feeling an unseen Grip. Whatever It was. Pure evil wrapped in lies. Clawing at him.

His thoughts trailed off into a desperate wonder: How could he stand alone without the Bourbies? They had become his bastion, his fortitude. And then, as is common with divers, he thoughtfully considered: Was all he'd become merely a fragile scaffolding held up by them? Or did it stand alone? Could *he* stand alone?

Willie had never felt so powerless. Verses of *Sagelia* attempted to rise within him but were soon wrestled down by the Grip. He lumbered toward the bench like a weary pugilist reeling from a staggering blow. *His* bench. The one nestled beneath the boughs of the Twinkleleaf Ash, where it all began. He needed to quell the storm within.

He closed his eyes. As his senses retreated into a muted embrace, a window within his soul creaked open. A torrent of memories surged forward. Recollections of desolate times as a young orphan when his simple yearnings to be cherished, understood, and regarded remained unfulfilled. Those years were a relentless tug-of-war. A struggle to relinquish what time and again proved to be mere harbingers of anguish.

Despite his attempts to cast away those desires, Willie couldn't shake them. Suppressing them meant settling for mere existence. A half-life. Walking about a world drawn with black-and-white lines. Devoid of color, texture, or movement. In his depths, he just understood something beyond his current state. Or, we should say, *in* his state.

Just as one freezing at night amplifies his anticipation of warmth in the rising sun, so in the depths of Willie's privation was a resilient hope for provision. Hinting at a destiny waiting to be fulfilled. Intimating the presence of

Someone. Memories surged with the unwavering vitality of the Taddy Torrent, echoing an unspoken Whisper: "You were there. As was I. And I am now here. And will forever be."

Willie suddenly *felt* McPorcinski's voice rise from somewhere in his depths. It came with a vivid memory of something that took place on one particularly monumental day. After their usual convivial merry-making, sensing a shadow's long hold over his little friend, the elder beckoned Willie to remain a little longer. Dispensing another wee nip of bourbon, eyes gleaming with such attentive, solemn care, McPorcinski seemed to look directly into Willie's soul. A door of inter-piglet depth the likes of which he'd never known was suddenly open.

As the hours passed, McPorcinski confided some of his ordeals as a lad in the harrowing Pitchfork Wars. For Willie, such was the thing of school study, far removed from his remotest understanding. In the midst of the most trying and even horrific travails, McPorcinski intimated how something else was happening, something truly remarkable that would not have happened had he not been in such a fiery cauldron. He hadn't simply survived; he'd thrived.

I cannot underestimate how momentous that day was for our beloved friend, Willie. Something dormant in him came alive. An insight. A perspective. Life-transforming wisdom that external circumstances, as turbulent as they might be, held significantly less sway over his life than the perspective he chose to adopt. The Grip always leveled Its attack in vulnerable, trying times. Presenting itself as all-powerful. A solution. Even a consolation. But It was merely an imposter. A pretender. With malicious intent. And most consequentially, with no real power.

So there Willie was, his depths caught up in an eddy spun by his friends' absence. It was as if his beloved mentor was there, speaking with commanding certitude: *Willie, you are the sovereign of your depths. You are destined for something great. You alone have the power to choose. Just as in the past, so it is in the present.* Amid the greatest tumult, powerless over external circumstances, peering inside, Willie could identify the despicable, deceiving voice of the Grip, the Pretender. And then, at these crossroads, Willie became quite convinced that he, and he alone, had the power to decide in his story if he would be written as a victim or the victor.

A hint of a smile broke forth from his soul and slowly reversed the sullen lines of his face.

From the sage-like witness of the Bourbies, Willie had come to learn that wisdom was, first and foremost, a mirror. A true mirror. Revealing his true nature. Not some grotesque thing fabricated by jaded experiences, obscured by clouds, or fractured by fiction. A true mirror reveals what each of us most fundamentally is: a breath of the Whisper, transcending all that is transient and fleeting. Gazing into this true mirror revealed resplendent truths capable of dispelling shadows across all time and space.

On this battlefield, knowing the power of words to summon otherwise unseen warriors into the arena, Willie began softly mumbling declarations. "Depart from me, Pretender!" and "You have no authority!" and "I banish you! I am the sovereign!" In doing this, he tapped some courageous capacity in his soul, releasing a power he'd never experienced. As his declarations grew in conviction, trickles became streams pouring forth with the force of the mighty Taddy Torrent. He could feel the gnarly, clenched knuckles of the Grip giving way at his command.

What a humorous sight it was to behold this peculiar little piglet, jaunty cap askew, little hooves racing about Pigletsville Square as if holding a lit firework with its rapidly depleting fuse, just trying to find a clandestine place where he might explode. He went here and then there, frantically crossing streets, raising more than a few eyebrows. His now hot little hooves finally landed him just behind Trotters Tap House, where the mighty current of the Taddy Torrent flowed, white foam galloping downstream like herds of wild horses. It seemed to reach inside and connect with whatever was in him.

Brought there, so mindful of standing before the pernicious

power of the Grip, mindful of the havoc It had caused, with all the forceful rage he could muster towards this now unveiled specter, Willie burst out with a declarative power that seemed to echo throughout the surrounding hills: "YOU… HAVE… NO… AUTHORITY! I BANISH YOU!"

Falling to his knees in absolute exhaustion, tears streaming down his face, he breathed what felt like his first breath. An incredible freedom surged within him that he had never known. Which is to say, a horizon of freedom he didn't know existed. The Grip was gone. Banished. Willie just knelt there, caught up in the formidable force flowing from Maiden Falls.

I don't think this can be overemphasized. Over time, entire kingdoms rise and fall, but none come close to the power of one piglet assuming sovereignty over the kingdom of his own soul. So, dear reader, please allow me one more reverberation. Up to this point, Willie was like a freestyle climber who, exerting all his strength, frantically grasping upward against jagged rocks, feels at the bitter end, reaches deep inside, and summons all his remaining strength in one final, desperate leap. Only to find himself peering just over the summit. Filled with an exhilarating freedom he had never known, with adrenaline coursing through him, he pulls himself up.

Now standing tall at the top of the conquered height, he looks down at where he'd been. The vast expanse of it. The things he'd run from. Or buried. So many things he'd allowed to fester under the tyranny of the Grip. And right then, it occurred to him he was wrong in presuming that rising above required severing one's roots. He was no longer afraid of them. He need not regard his past as some sort of fiend ever trying to rob him of his present. He need not keep his most difficult memories locked in a cage holding him captive.

A sparkle radiated from Willie as bright as a hundred luminous Flutterbees dancing on a moonless night. Emboldened, looking squarely in this invisible mirror, gazing at the horizon, Willie felt the exuberance of being fully in command on his throne.

From this height, as the torrent of memories cascaded, Willie no longer perceived himself as an abandoned orphan with a hollow emptiness in his soul; instead, he recognized a distinctive void meant to be filled. He became aware of an unseen Hoof guiding him all along, from that vacuous space inside to a place at the table of the Bourby Gambit Guild. In the depths of his being, he believed that same unseen Hoof was guiding him at that very moment. And would continue to do so.

CHAPTER 8
Echoes of Silence

Just as sure as a Squigglesprout seed breaks forth from the cold, entombing earth and, with each passing day, begins to unfold its petals before the radiance of the morning sun, so Willie had found his sure roots in the convivial friendship of the Bourbies. He wasn't adrift; he was precisely where he was meant to be—a sturdy foundation from which he could unfurl his wings. Yet, as thoughts of his cherished friends weighed heavily upon him, questions lingered about their fate, wrapped in the silent embrace of an unspoken Whisper: "You were there. As was I. And as I am now here. And will forever be."

At this sacred bench, Willie opened his eyes, newfound assurance coursing through him. Amid the haunting array of empty chairs scattered before him, his gaze fixated on a peculiar sight—a solitary pawn standing resolutely at the heart of a chessboard, forsaken by all else. This singular symbol, which he had come to identify with so deeply, seemed to declare to all the abyssal gloom swirling about him, "I may be small, but I will not fall!"

With confidence, resolute but solemn, Willie reached for the cherished piece, feeling its familiar weight in his palm, a tangible representation of the bonds that connected him to the Bourby Gambit Guild. Clenching it tightly, his fingers traced the smooth contours, imprinting its significance upon his heart. He gazed at it, his eyes reflecting a blend of sorrow and determination, a silent acknowledgment of the unseen guidance woven through his life.

He tenderly placed the pawn in his pocket, a gesture imbued with affection and reverence, a silent promise to carry forward the mission it symbolized. A gentle pat, a token of gratitude, sealed the moment—a cherished remnant of the past now nestled close to his soul as a guiding reminder of the Whisper's enduring presence.

The surge of fervor within him emanated from an unshakable foundation of truth, never to be sacrificed on the altar of sentiment. This stirring wasn't meant solely to move him; it was the wind in his sails, compelling him to move.

The battle against darkness is not won in shadows. The most luminous light in a soul is of no consequence if it remains hidden. Within him was a new battle. A new struggle. A new realm of protest. While he felt himself standing solidly on a summit, he also felt unspoken fear ascending with the sharpness of a thousand tacks around him. He felt helpless again. His meager voice, once having a magnetism to move mountains, was diminished and drowned in the overwhelming tide of manipulation by the Grip.

Willie raised a silent plea, "What shall I do?" With no discernable reply coming from any depths or heights, he knew the answer. Just keep doing it. It's all he knew. So he did. Every day, peddling papers, though he was more and more aware of being a cog in the wheel. Cherished truths were crumbling under the spell of Deep Pen. He'd close his eyes a hundred times a day and beckon, "What else? What else? What else?" More often, accompanied by "Why? Why? Why?" Despite his silent prayers to the Whisper and humming the *Ballad of Sagelia*, he was left with no reply.

CHAPTER 9
RISE OF THE SHATTERGLASS SCALLYWAGS

ll along this descent into darkness, no one seemed to notice the most sweet and beautiful voice of the Squigglesprouts eerily absent; even the brightest days seemed devoid of radiance. The pressure mounted as the disappearance of beloved piglets continued. Each absence deepened the fear, pushing those who resisted into shadows, seeking shelter from the menacing murk. Conversations simmered in hushed tones, questioning the once-relied-upon beacons of truth in the news. The very fabric of their understanding was fraying, leaving them adrift in an ocean of uncertainty.

Yet amidst this turmoil, Willie's unassuming demeanor at the center of town belied a resilience and depth that attracted some who knew and resisted Deep Pen's grip. Around Willie, a sort of network of divers emerged: piglets bound together, having been forged for depth. Attentive to the Whisper, with renewed enthusiasm in singing the *Ballad* when together or alone, they beheld truth, allowing them to navigate the murky waters of deceit. Mindful that they were being watched and rounded up by Deep Pen's secret agents, they exercised extreme caution.

So it was after a few weeks of secretly gathering regularly in Willie's apartment at the far corner of Pigletsville Square that, cloaked in the cover of midnight (when Joe Wolf and his minions were suspiciously absent), they began with their usual soft humming of the *Ballad of Sagelia*. Then Aldus "Porky" Porksmith, with the mischief of a thousand Glitterwhirls, reached into his frumpy coat and declared, "I hereby bequeath to thee, me, one, and all..." and, producing a bottle of the rare Hog Haven Reserve bourbon, continued, "the true Sqweak Sauce!" Followed by, "The distinguished drink of deplorables!"

Explosive laughter and "Hear, hear!" broke out, painting the scene with the colorful exuberance of pigs in the mud pit at a Snoutball Festival. To the immeasurable delight of all present, while dispensing ample portions of the cherished beverage, "Porky" continued, "Now then, this intrepid assemblage of porcine rebels needs a moniker!" Smiles proclaimed a welcome change in atmosphere, from creeping desolation to one of delight.

Names summarily bounced about like a pail of ping-pong balls dumped on the floor: "Trotters' Alliance!" "Porcine Protectors!" "Oink Brigade!" Riffing off one another with the virtuosity of real friendship, if a particularly fine point was made, "Hortens" Hortenschlager would shout gaily, "Scallywag!" followed by a sip of bourbon. In the peculiar way rituals develop among friends, the others quickly joined this, following any point, or no point at all with: "Scallywag!" Of course, this was chased by a sip of bourbon.

Such a healing and transforming thing all this was! All the conviviality, revelry, and all the rest spoke of belonging and friendship: the very currency of inter-piglet depth. The grandest pursuit and prized possession of every piglet. Characterizing our magnificent piglets in their original state.

As you might imagine, such revelry, which went on for quite some time, left them exhausted. The embrace of unspoken words wrapped around them with the warmth of their crackling fire. Such a grand silence captivated their souls beyond that of any symphony. Just as the comforting arms of slumber were beginning to reach for them, Willie's voice broke the tranquil hush. "About the name...."

Well, this reignited a fresh wave of laughter. Yet, within the mirth, a solemnity emerged where the gravity of their gathering pressed upon them. Eager for levity but tethered by the seriousness of their intent, they turned their attention to their revered leader, all ears perked in reverent quietude, ready to name their porcine revolution.

With profound sincerity, Willie spoke. "It feels like we're *in* the *Ballad*." Landy Murfield, still mildly inebriated, added, "Yeaaah. I'd just like to... shaaaatter glasssss... the mirror that Saaageeelia... you know...." Following some snickers, Briggs McConnelly chimed in: "Sagelia. She shattered Shadowglass. We are the Shatterglass Scallywags." With joyous smiles, all expressed their approval by raising a glass and shouting, "Scallywag!" And so they came to be the Shatterglass Scallywags. Their mission, to shatter the Deep Pen Syndicate's evil reign.

Each gathering fueled the Scallywags with an unwavering resolve to halt the rapidly progressing disassembly line, and to awaken their bewitched Pigletsville, regardless of the cost. Together, they became adept at discerning truth from fiction, united by their determination to unravel Deep Pen's tangled web of deceit. They delved into the origins and intent behind the Wuham Virus and adamantly resisted the weaponization of Sqweak Sauce.

The information being assembled by Willie and his companions was substantial, with the capacity to expose the nefarious Deep Pen. The Scallywags remained an extraordinary threat to The Syndicate. They knew they were being surveilled. They needed a hero. They needed someone powerful enough to withstand the juggernaut. Someone who could rally them.

With his keen sensibilities, Willie knew who it must be. Amid the chaos, whispers of a mysterious figure fluttered through the town. Deep Pen's controlled papers consistently defamed this enigmatic character, painting him in hues of malice and darkness. But something about it all sparked a glimmer of hope within Willie as he sensed a flicker of goodness, a beacon amidst the blight. It was a hope born from desperation, a fragile thread that wove through his heart, yearning to stand against the tide and revive the lost truths that were slipping through their grasp.

And Willie knew where. He must go to the epicenter of the most malevolent machinations of Deep Pen. Whatever it was called before, it was now regarded as New Pork. Where the shadow lingered like a moonless night. Where Sqweak Sauce was poured out on tap. Where nearly the entire populace was under the trance of Deep Pen. He must make the perilous journey, knowing Deep Pen was tracking his every move. Willie hoped to find and connect with the man simply referred to as The Do.

To avoid suspicion, the Scallywags reluctantly agreed that he needed to go alone. Briggs McConnelly, the closest in size, would don his clothes and maintain his paperboy duties.

CHAPTER 10
UNSEEN CLASH OF SWORDS

I
n unseen depths, a fierce clash of swords was reverberating in the atmosphere, thrusts being met with parries. At Split Tree, before the bastion of the bloodthirsty wolves, Draven Blackclaw sardonically intoned, "Joe Wolf." His voice had a sinister cadence that resonated through the ancient trees like a foreboding incantation, each syllable dripping with a venomous hiss that mirrored the predatory intent within. His eyes, gleaming like shards of obsidian, fixated on Joe Wolf with an intensity that penetrated the darkness. The ambient glow of his predatory gaze betrayed an otherworldly intelligence, as if the very shadows themselves whispered their secrets into his keen ears.

"There is a disturbance," he continued, the words hanging in the air like a spectral premonition. The forest seemed to respond, the rustling leaves and distant howls attuned to the dissonance that had disrupted the wolves' malevolent cacophony. "A dissonance that threatens to unravel the fabric of our grand design."

Joe Wolf, the obedient puppet, shifted uncomfortably, his features contorted into an uneasy expression. "I assure you, Master, I've deployed our agents to uncover any threat to our plans. No pigpen remains unmuddied."

The foreboding leader fixed his piercing gaze on Joe Wolf, a silent warning lingering in the air. "This disturbance is not to be underestimated. It is an anomaly that eludes even my watchful eye. Failure to quell this discord could jeopardize everything we've worked for."

Joe Wolf, sensing the gravity of the situation, nodded fervently. "I will redouble our efforts. No threat shall escape our scrutiny. Pigletsville will be overtaken." With a final, stern warning, Draven Blackclaw dismissed Joe Wolf to carry out the imperative task of identifying and suppressing the elusive disturbance.

CHAPTER 11
Escape to New Pork

Having discovered that the wolves would be preoccupied at midnight when their nefarious Wolven Conclaves took place at the Split Tree, Willie set out for a mysterious, distant, darkest, far-reaching corner rumored to have some connection to Pigletsville, understood to be the very bastion of Deep Pen, New Pork. Each step was veiled in secrecy, moving only under the cover of night while hiding in the daylight's wake.

Days elapsed without food or much sleep. Exhaustion and hunger gnawed at his spirit. Having made his way slowly, cautiously through another night, just as the first rays of light began painting a majestic horizon, Willie welcomed the graceful embrace of a towering Willowhistle, its ancient boughs offering secrecy and safety. Collapsing upon the verdant bed of leaves and branches, weariness conquered him swiftly, drawing him into deep slumber.

As the sun arced its course across the heavens, Willie's dreams held him rapt in a surreal waltz of terror and solace.

Fragments of his orphaned past emerged like flickering candlelight in a dim-lit room. He glimpsed the desolate streets where he wandered as a young piglet, his heart aching with the pang of loneliness, yearning for warmth and kinship. Then, the ethereal veil transitioned to brighter scenes—the jubilant moments when he encountered the Bourbies. And in the way of dreams, these friends became a field of Squigglesprouts, filling him with the exuberance of belonging.

Then, while basking in the warm summer light among his companions, with the sudden impact of thunder splitting the sky, it seemed that a floor gave way, leaving him in the horror of free-falling into the chilling embrace of an endless void. Reaching out frantically, he grasped at the muddied earth lining his descent, clawing at it helplessly, terrified at the immanence of a certain fate. Only then did he find himself caught up in a gentle breeze and suddenly flying in an odd contraption. His Scallywag friends, each piloting their own, were filled with merriment, shouting to one another with delight, drawing attention to their various maneuvers.

This bliss was abruptly overtaken by a forsaken forest where Willie found himself running in terror, in a way that seemed endless, being pursued by a specter of vicious fangs veiled in shadows with unspeakable howls, paws ever-pounding with his racing heart, getting closer and closer. At some point, Willie could hear the terrified cries of his friends, always beyond his reach. Willie came to a vast clearing to behold a large gathering of the most hideous-looking wolves gathered about a great fire.

Filled with trepidation, hiding behind a tree, he strained to see the object of their ferocity; just fifty yards away, he could make out images of his beloved friends, mouths gagged, hooves held fast, and being violently hoisted up by ropes, upside-down and suspended above the fire. Terrified, feeling helpless, and ashamed, he was just about ready to run; he felt the sharpness of a wolven paw heavy on his shoulder accompanied by a sardonic scowl. "Why, hello there."

Chilled with sweat and shaking uncontrollably, Willie was suddenly roused by a kindly voice. "Well, what have we here?

Me tree seems to be quite fond of ye, but ye seem to have lost yer way, laddie! Me name's McPorcinski!" The elder soul's words summarily vanquished the horror, a voice laden with goodness and wisdom that stirred echoes of familiarity within Willie's heart. All this happened just as the sun was bidding its farewell. He had slept the entire day.

Hearing the name "McPorcinski" sparked a warm flow of tenderness within him, washing away any suspicion. Though not an exact match to his cherished Bourby friend, the likeness more than hinted at a kinship, a shared thread with the same features. As they exchanged familiar references, Willie's heart swelled with a mixture of joy and sorrow – this was, unmistakably, McPorcinski's younger brother, a revelation that soothed and ached within him. Their conversation seamlessly spanned the adversities under Joe Wolf and Deep Pen, punctuated by McPorcinski's colorful curses.

Shortly after that, Willie found himself in the solace of a crackling fire within McPorcinski's humble abode before a veritable feast of the choicest fruit, bread, nuts, and many other delights, and a wee spot of the best bourbon he'd ever had. Words of hope, strength, and the *Ballad of Sagelia* reverberated within those walls. Sleep again reached out and embraced Willie in its benevolent arms.

The next thing Willie knew, it was morning. They must have left him sleeping before the fire. Mrs. McPorcinski gently tapped his shoulder. As his eyes adjusted, Willie was struck by the grim looks staring back at him. Mr. McPorcinski somberly placed the *New Pork Times* on his lap. There on the front page, just above a photo of his Scallywag companions, was the damning headline, "Dangerous Terrorist Cell Dismantled," with the byline, "Leader still at large," and quotes branding them as "deplorables."

A sinking began to envelop Willie's heart. He felt as though he might faint. He read the accusations, each word striking like a hammer on an anvil of disbelief. The paper painted him as a callous conspirator, even accusing him of the deaths of "elderly chess-playing piglets." Willie couldn't breathe. All air was knocked out of him. His mind was spinning. Did this mean his beloved Bourby friends were killed?

A profound silence descended upon them, suffocating the air, broken only by a single tear tracing Willie's cheek before a downpour of uncontrollable sobs. He buried his face in his folded arms on the table, his shoulders convulsing in sorrow. His very essence mourned for his friends. McPorcinski, a solid hoof still resting on Willie's shoulder, remained a steadfast presence, offering earnest consolation.

In a daze of disbelief and concern, Willie's eyes darted back to the paper, the sidebar glaring at him like a warning beacon: "The Do Back in the Pen." It felt like a punch to the gut. The weight of it all settled heavily on his shoulders. He couldn't shake the feeling of being trapped in some surreal nightmare where the lines between reality and fantasy blurred with every passing moment.

It was only a few moments later when, in the throes of what seemed to be inconsolable despair, Willie reached for his pocket. Became aware of its cherished occupant. He took out the pawn. Held it in his hooves. Right at that moment, all at once, McPorcinski, who knew none of what was happening, was stirred by the abrupt change in Willie's countenance, a change in the atmosphere. A palpable, monumental power began to radiate from his peculiar little friend. From such an unassuming thing. He wondered but didn't dare ask. And in that, he beheld the mystery. Engulfed in shadows, Willie was before the mirror. Seeing who he was. A palpable power stirred within him. A reservoir of strength drawn from an unseen wellspring of determination. "You were there. As was I. And as I am now here. And will forever be."

In that fleeting instant, Willie knew his course. He wiped away his tears and bid farewell to his heartful hosts. The resolve crystallized within him—he would find the incarcerated leader. Willie had to reach The Do to unveil the truth, hoping his words would not fall on deaf ears.

CHAPTER 12
The Weight of Shadows

In the eerie glow of moonlight filtering through the dense foliage of Split Tree, Draven Blackclaw, silhouetted against the encircling gloom, convened the inner council of Deep Pen in the usual way. "If it looks like a piglet, but eats a piglet," he intoned with a discernible note of apprehension, if not concern. The atmosphere crackled with an electric tension, palpable in the hushed whispers and anxious glances exchanged between the assembled leaders whose ritual response, "It's a wolf," was somewhat exasperated, and completely devoid of the sinister huckstering.

"Brothers of The Syndicate," Draven's voice echoed through the clearing, each word laden with gravitas. "We stand at a precipice, teetering on the edge of uncertainty."

The wolves exchanged knowing looks, their eyes reflecting the flickering firelight as Draven continued, his voice a low growl of determination. "Our pet, Joe Wolf, once a stalwart sentinel of our nefarious designs, has begun to falter. His once-sharp mind, a weapon wielded with precision, has dulled like a blade left to rust."

A murmur of agreement rippled through the council, punctuated by the occasional snarl of frustration. "He's forgetting his place," one wolf muttered, his hackles raised in agitation.

"Indeed," Draven nodded solemnly. "Joe Wolf's decline jeopardizes the delicate balance of our entire operation. His diminishing mental acuity has become a liability, a ticking time bomb waiting to detonate."

"But what of the tether?" another wolf interjected, his voice tinged with apprehension. "Has he forgotten our connection to the Wolven overlords?"

Draven's gaze darkened, his eyes flashing with a dangerous intensity. "He forgets at our peril," he growled. "He is being seen. A liability we can ill afford."

Silence descended upon the clearing, broken only by the crackling of the fire and the rustling of leaves in the night breeze. Each council member absorbed the weight of Draven's words, the gravity of their situation hanging heavy in the air like a shroud.

"We must act swiftly," Draven declared, his voice cutting through the stillness like a blade. Scratching his whiskery chin with nervous intensity, he continued, "We cannot allow Joe Wolf's decline to jeopardize everything we have worked so tirelessly to achieve."

The council nodded in silent agreement; their resolve hardened like steel. In the shadows of Split Tree, amid whispered conspiracies and whispered fears, the fate of Deep Pen hung in the balance.

All returned the next midnight to the dimly-lit clearing at Split Tree with one more present. The weight of Deep Pen's expectations bore down heavily upon Joe Wolf, their once-prominent prodigy. For years, they had groomed him, sculpting his image and orchestrating his every move to serve their sinister agenda. But as the years wore on and the burden grew heavier, Joe Wolf was crumbling beneath the weight of his own sinister work.

"Joe, you've served us well," Draven Blackclaw, the cunning mastermind behind Deep Pen, spoke with a tone that dripped with sinister satisfaction. "But it's time for a change."

Joe Wolf's weary eyes met Draven's cold gaze, the heavy burden of his exhaustion evident in the droop of his eyelids and the lines etched deep into his furrowed brow. Each word he spoke seemed to weigh heavily on his tongue, as if the effort of forming coherent sentences depleted what little energy remained within him.

"I've done everything you've asked of me," Joe Wolf replied, his voice a mere whisper amidst the crackling of the nearby flames, heavy with defeat and the weariness of a soul stretched thin beyond its limits. His words hung in the air like a shroud, punctuating the toll exacted by his relentless service to Deep Pen.

But beyond the physical fatigue and cognitive fog that clouded his mind, something deeper lurked, something intangible yet palpable—a gnawing sense of something fundamentally and gravely *wrong*. It was a silent torment that clawed at his very core, whispering of unspoken doubts and fears that he dared not acknowledge.

Draven's lips curled into a twisted smirk, the glint of malice in his eyes casting shadows that danced across Joe's weary countenance. "We understand, Joe. But you've outlived your usefulness to us," he declared, his words like a dagger piercing through the fragile facade of Joe's resilience. "And you know what happens to those who outlive their usefulness."

As the weight of Draven's words settled upon him like a leaden cloak, Joe felt the ground shift beneath his feet, the once-familiar landscape of his existence now rendered unfamiliar and hostile. It was a moment of reckoning, a realization that his fate was no longer his own to control, but rather a pawn in the sinister machinations of those who held sway over Deep Pen's destiny.

The air was thick with tension and foreboding; the fate of Joe Wolf teetered on the brink. Drawing upon their recognition of his long-established political significance and strategic positioning within Pigletsville, his words trembled with fear and resignation. "But who shall take my place? How shall we crush the rebellion?" In the deafening silence that followed, Joe felt himself slipping into the dark abyss of their icy stares. With his head hanging like a wilting flower in the shadow of a looming storm, a final, defeated plea escaped with all the force of a whimper, "Please. Please. How else might I serve my master?"

After a pregnant pause, Blackclaw's countenance suddenly shifted, marked by a sardonic spark of new consideration in his eyes. His brows furrowed as if grappling with a revelation; his gaze flickered with a calculated intensity. With a subtle nod to the other wolves encircling the fire, he straightened his posture as if solidifying his resolve. Locking eyes with Joe, Blackclaw addressed his council. "Though he may be withering like a leaf, there is still blood yet to cull before his descent," he declared, punctuating his words with sinister snickers.

Joe Wolf's heart sank as he realized the true nature of Draven's plan. While his late plea momentarily spared him from a worse fate, he would be replaced as mayor, discarded like a worn-out toy, his legacy reduced to a mere asterisk in the annals of Deep Pen's history. He was expendable, a mere cog in their grand machine. They cared not for his well-being nor the toll their machinations' took on him. All that mattered was preserving their power, even if it meant sacrificing one of their own. In the end, he was but a pawn in their game, a casualty of their insatiable lust for control.

In the days that followed, it seemed like every mistake, every difficulty, every problem that could not be shielded from the piglet populace was hoisted upon the fragile shoulders of Joe Wolf. Where in the past, PNN and the *New Pork Times* would bend over backward to dismiss all these guffaws, selectively casting its light only on the "deplorables," on any who would question the narrative that did not correspond to The Syndicate, it was now evident that something had been decided.

CHAPTER 13
PAWN OF GREAT POWER

B raced with thoughts of his mission and his loyal companions, Willie marched steadfastly towards the glistening spires of New Pork looming in the distance. Upon reaching the city's outskirts, he encountered an impenetrable fortress guarded by the watchful eyes of Deep Pen. Time seemed to elude his grasp, urging him to act swiftly.

Approaching the nearest gate, Willie addressed the guards with unyielding conviction and calmness that made his greeting amusing. "I am Willie. The dangerous criminal you seek. Head of the Shatterglass Scallywags. Take me in." Completely caught off guard, thinking him just a few apples short of a bushel, they broke into contemptuous laughter.

At that moment, Willie's gaze pierced beyond the superficial facades, recognizing his fellow creatures not as adversaries but as kindred souls, meant for magnificence yet ensnared in the web of manipulation. A sudden sorrow washed over him, akin to a plunge into icy waters, jolting him from the trance of division and hostility.

In the next moment, a flicker of determination ignited within him. His heart pulsated with a desire to shatter the chains of captivity that bound them, to reveal the truth obscured by deception. For Willie knew that true liberation lay in the gentle unveiling of each piglet's innate magnificence, reflected in the unfragmented mirror of their own hearts. Despite the lingering influence of the elusive Grip, which had once clouded his vision and tempted him to view others as mere adversaries, Willie now saw through its veil, recognizing the shared inter-piglet depths that bound them all.

From these depths, robust streams began to flow, filling him with such loving boldness. He had a deep desire to reach these warped piglets. He began drawing them beyond the shallows with thoughtful, clear questions. Questions that demanded answers. Questions exposing inconsistencies. He invited them to consider where they'd been versus where they were now. The truth of it all. About Joe Wolf. Deep Pen. Wuham. Sqweak Sauce. Who was in control. Who was pulling the strings. To what end. All of it.

Disarmed by his genuineness, under the command of unshakeable truth, perhaps stunned by his audacity, they allowed him to go on. He could feel those streams from within now overflowing, assailing the lies. He could feel their defenses slipping, punctuated by side glances and uncomfortable shifting from one hoof to another. He knew he was awakening something in their depths. Something that had been lulled to sleep. Something good and true.

But then, out of nowhere, he sensed in their leader a stronghold of shallows. A monolithic, evil thing that would move no further. Shackled by lies. Uncritically beholden to the doctrine of PNN, regardless of how many times and how many ways it contradicted itself. He sensed the fear of Deep Pen reprisal. Then this leader snapped: "All deplorable conspiracy!" The others joined in a rising clamor of contemptuous rage. They arrested Willie and followed their orders to bring him to the notorious prison in the very heart of New Pork.

While in terrible conditions and deprived of food, the worst of it was walls plastered with pages of the *New Pork Times* and the constantly streaming programming of PNN. Day and night. Without stop. Propaganda veiled as objective news. Day after day, they asked Willie the same questions, promising freedom if he would sign their bogus declarations. When such wasn't working, they issued threats. Were it not for their fear of Willie's connection to formidable information, it might have gone much worse.

Amid the relentless passage of days, apprehension gripped Willie's heart as he confronted the looming stakes. A sudden shock reverberated through him when he found himself face to face with none other than Joe Wolf, pretending to be something like a benevolent uncle who feigned understanding, care, and friendship. In an attempt to sway the piglet to his side, Joe employed artful persuasion.

Undeterred by Willie's resilience on the second day, Joe escalated his tactics, tempting him with opulent promises of every possession, power, and position conceivable for a piglet. As the allure of material enticements failed to break Willie's resolve, Joe, on the third day, feigned a moment of confiding intimacy. He whispered of Deep Pen's horrifying intentions, a chilling revelation encapsulated in a single word: "Sizzle."

Stripped of allies, utterly vulnerable to the sardonic forces closing in around him, Willie found himself swallowed by the oppressive omen. And yet it was on this night, living with an increasing clamoring of inmates and commotion, that Willie heard a very distinctive voice up the cell block. Almost immediately, something within him told him who it was. The man he'd traveled so far to find. The one most hated by Deep Pen.

Almost certain of the fate awaiting him, and running out of options and feeling completely constrained in this prison, Willie bowed his head and, out of nervousness, inadvertently reached for his pocket. Upon contact, something powerful surged within him. A reminder. His mirror. Not fractured or obscured. Taking him deep. Very deep. He slowly, solemnly pulled out the beloved object and, tears forming in his eyes, held it close to his heart.

As if summoned from the unseen realms, a gentle breeze moved with the noble grace of a celestial maiden's dance within Willie's prison cell, caressing him intimately with a whisper that transcended mere air. This clandestine visitor penetrated the depths of his being, setting aglow the dormant embers of memories past. The essence of Sagelia, the embodiment of all that was true, good, and magnificent about the piglets, unfolded before him, not as a mere recollection but as a profound encounter that transcended language.

In the embrace of this mysterious breeze, Willie felt an unmistakable presence, the ethereal manifestation of Sagelia herself. Her sweet voice reassured and encouraged him, a celestial chorus joining her and resonating with ancient whispers. It was the souls of those who had braved opposition and adversity throughout the ages. Their luminance, radiant as a thousand suns, flooded his soul with newfound clarity.

This set his soul ablaze and, clutching the pawn in his hoof as if it were Sagelia's Ancestral Stick before Shadowglass, Willie felt an irresistible urge to hum the *Ballad of Sagelia*, which quickly burst into song. The sweet melody, with its power to dispel the darkest night, echoed within the prison walls. As Willie's voice resounded, the inmates, ensnared in their murmurs and grumbles, found solace in the song. Something transcendent captured their collective consciousness, pushing aside any lingering thoughts. Among them was the one Willie sought to reach, the man holding the key to igniting hope among the piglets.

Gradually, an extraordinary transformation unfolded. With each repetition of the song, Willie infused it with increasing boldness and love, reaching into the hearts of all the inmates. A profound liberation ensued as they joined the chorus, the prison cell resonating with a consuming warmth that seemed to melt the cold, steel walls.

Now, this song powerfully struck the wolf guards in a different way, stirring up a ferocity fueling their venomous hatred. They frantically dispatched every available guard to Willie's cell. As these descended upon him with all their ravenous fury, violently threatening everyone else along the way to cease, the once-boisterous chorus of criminals began to subside. But not Willie.

Embracing the pawn as if it were part of his being, Willie remained so calm. The sweet melody kept reverberating from his little lungs. It was almost as if he were in another realm, oblivious to the violence that was about to be visited upon him.

The savage pack swung his cell door open with a thunderous clang, followed by an indescribable uproar of vicious howls echoing throughout the dank, desolate walls, sending shivers down the spines of all who witnessed the scene unfolding before them.

And all at once, the sweet, sweet, beautiful ballad went silent.

An eerie stillness hung heavy in the air like a suffocating blanket. The malevolence retreated, revealing a scene of profound tragedy etched in the cold, unforgiving stone of the cell floor. A newsboy cap in tatters, once-faded, was now brightly colored by the stain of blood. And incredible bravery. Next to a small, battered, lifeless, beautiful little body. One hoof still clinging to a treasure beyond compare.

The diminutive, magnificent pawn had given his life. For a king.

Based entirely upon the assumption of a shallow self-preservation and selfishness, the Sizzilian Protocol had not anticipated this. The atmosphere that, just moments before, was under an ominous shadow of something profane had suddenly and surreptitiously become something sacred. Consumed by a presence beyond words or reckoning. Piercing into depths many of them hadn't known existed. You might say, liberating inner prisoners and setting captives free.

A solemn reverence of a thousand grand cathedrals filled the prison, a silent tribute to a fallen hero. For in that moment, as the echoes of violence faded into the darkness, Willie's sacrifice resonated with a power that transcended death itself—the enduring legacy of truth discovered and lived.

Somewhere amid the brooding clouds veiling the once-noble land, a haunting sound emerged from a solitary flower whose voice was thought to be extinguished. The dirge echoed with mourning as deep as an ocean and permeated the air with a celestial sweetness that overcame the foul breezes looming over Pigletsville. Slowly but surely, majestic petals unfolding before the sun, this solitary, diminutive voice became two. Two became many. Shadowglass was struck. Squigglesprout was reborn.

CHAPTER 14
The Torch Is Passed

In this somber moment, let us linger and feel the weight of the loss, allowing our tears to intertwine with the mighty Maiden Falls cascading into the vibrant Taddy Torrent. The melodious sounds of Squigglesprout accompany this tragic departure, demanding more than fleeting acknowledgment. This is a moment for the wise hands of mourning and sorrow to mold us. Alas, dear reader, a customary funeral procession will not unfold here. Not in the public gaze, not in the shallows. Instead, prepare for a resonance far more magnificent.

Now, if a storyteller might be allowed a moment of over-the-top flourish, this would be it. The subject demands it.

In this tenebrous tapestry, a flicker of hope emerged from an unexpected hero—Don Hairdo, or The Do. Before delving into the profundity of this appellation, let us revel in a moment of levity. Named for his resplendent mane, each strand seemingly caressed by the very zephyrs that grace his presence, The Do's follicular marvel was more than a coiffure; it transformed into a proclamation, an exclamation mark, a manifesto heralding, "I have arrived to make the pen great again!"

Charismatic and affluent, The Do had been standing at the intersection of fortune and adversity—ever endeavoring to free his fellow piglet populace from the clutches of manipulation and oppression, but besieged by Narcissyndrome, a condition that, while challenging his sway over piglets ensnared by Deep Pen, rendered him impervious to its allure. While in his depths he had always sensed some amorphous fragility and was tormented by its presence, in the maligned nature of things, Narcissyndrome distorts one's view through a self-twisted lens, fostering a bitter defense mechanism against any challenge to the image. Thus, The Do generally accepted these things as essential to his nature, which kept him beholden to the Grip.

Deep Pen and their latest mayoral installment, Spamin Gruesome, greatly feared The Do's ability to rouse the masses from a delusional stupor and expose the Pen's wolven nature. Thus, in the whimsical arena of Pigletsville's political circus, a gripping showdown was ever unfolding. Gruesome was amplifying calls to imprison the charismatic Don Hairdo. As twisted legal calisthenics were proving insufficient, they continued to exploit his Achilles heel, Narcissyndrome, by manipulating news sources and leveraging Sqweak Sauce. Gruesome continued to twist his words, baiting him to respond. Blinded by his condition, The Do bit almost every time, erupting in combustible or disparaging ways.

Yet, in recent weeks, something had changed. Something was newly reverberating in the Do's soul. He could trace this back to what he now referred to as The Day. Specifically, during one of his ceremonial stays in New Pork Prison when, amidst a violent clamor, a sweet, small voice reverberated through the walls and haunted the souls of all present:

'NEATH NOBLE SKIES AND SHADOWS' PLIGHT,
IN PIGLETSVILLE'S SERENE MOONLIGHT.
SAGELIA, BLESSED, WITH EYES TO SEE,
FELT DISTRACTION'S DEADLY ENMITY.

A memory from childhood, perhaps from a grandparent or family friend, swept into his inner dissonance like a summer breeze through an open window.

> DIVERTUSIS, IN GUILE ARRAYED,
> WOVE DISCORD WITH A MASQUERADE.
> 'NEATH THE FULL MOON'S WATCHFUL GAZE,
> SAGELIA UNVEILED HIS WICKED WAYS.

Quelling the storm within, the *Ballad* became a melodic stream flowing into his depths. Awakening clarity. Before his true mirror, he saw his past ways, how he unwittingly became an accomplice to tendrils extending into his family and friendships. The sweet *Ballad* had risen in him like a magnificent sun, shattering his night with a resplendent dawn. There, he perceived clearly, as one sees a silhouette, the grotesque, defiant shape of the iron Grip; this Thing he had accepted as his identity, he now saw as a great imposter. A pretender to his throne.

The *Ballad* sparked a resolve to do good, inundating him with power surpassing ten thousand luminous Flutterbees. Summiting and gazing at life below, a whisper in his depths affirmed: "You were there. As was I. And as I am now here. And will forever be."

> A PACT IN SHADOWS, FORGED WITH CARE,
> TO SHIELD HER KIN FROM SHADOWS' SNARE.
> WITH ANCESTRAL STAFF, THROUGH DARKNESS TROD,
> SHATTERING ILLUSIONS, BREAKING THE FLAWED.

Amid the tempest of adversity, Hairdo's transformation was unfolding. Unbeknownst to the schemers, their attacks weren't consuming him but were purifying him. Adversity was forging his moral character, intensifying in strength. As Narcissyndrome's tendrils began to dissolve, a true leader was emerging—humble yet bold, compassionate yet unyielding, visionary yet grounded. The once-flawed leader was standing as an unassailable bulwark against the forces that plagued

Pigletsville. Far below the shallows of politics and social structures, Hairdo's metamorphosis was becoming a triumph for the entire village. Attacks intended to weaken him were kindling the flames of dedication to Pigletsville's welfare.

PIGLETSVILLE, ONCE VEILED IN NIGHT,
BY SAGELIA'S SACRIFICE, EMERGED IN LIGHT.
GUIDED BY THE WHISPER'S LORE,
MAGNIFICENT FOREVERMORE.

As surely as the sun rises, piglets were beginning to see their true mirror, awakening from their beguilement. As they were beginning to see through the lies of Spamin Gruesome, the sweet sound of Squigglesprouts and piglets singing *Sagelia* were beginning to reverberate once again. Deep Pen's hold was weakening. The Wolven Syndicate was beside itself, with horrific howls echoing throughout the midnight forests.

An epic showdown remained.

CHAPTER 15
A Tale of Triumph &
Tumultuous Echoes of Tomorrow

E mbarking upon Willie's epic odyssey, we have been awakened to the pernicious yet pretentious power of the Grip and Its forces ever vying for our allegiance. We have been stirred by self-discovery, standing before the veritable mirror of truth. The echoes of a meager pawn's remarkable sacrifice continue to resonate. And yet, we must pronounce that, on this side of *Somewhere*, such metamorphosis seldom achieves finality. The Grip never ceases seduction. Each piglet, free but wounded by captivity, ever dealing with the vestigial claws of a false identity, must be ever watchful and vigilant in identifying and evicting pretenders to the throne.

During the grand showdown, completely outside the bounds of the Sizzilian Protocol playbook, The Do, despite a profound awakening to his true self, finds himself enmeshed in the ongoing battle against shadows. Inspiring revolution, he stands as a beacon. Yet, at this moment, he grapples with the relentless advance, the full-blown ferocity, of Deep Pen. And so it is at this pivotal moment when, amidst a sea of Pigletsville patriots following a "Make the Pen Great Again" rally, a peculiar farrow of piglet lads approaches him.

Fighting back unseen waves of emotion, their new leader, Porky Porksmith, solemnly hands Don Hairdo a small box as if he were entrusting his very soul: "Mr. Do... please accept this. It was the price paid for...." Overcome by emotion, Porky bows his head under the weight, just trying to keep it together. Then, drawing strength from some reservoir within, he raises his eyes and, with a purity of conviction forged in unquenchable fire, Porky speaks directly to The Do's soul: "It was the price paid for your life by our beloved friend, Willie." Taking a breath, final words surge out of him as if a blessing from another realm. "He was with you then. He is with us now. And will forever be."

Later that night, as The Do continued to wrestle with so many things he could not see, he found himself drifting off into the comforting embrace of Great Silence—a reality meriting many pages if not volumes, its magnificence elucidated in the great works of Pigletsville philosophers long passed. For our purposes here, but a brief mention. How magnificent it is to be freed from the piercing edges that assail us, even if only for a moment. An occasion to be revived in streams of healing water, moving in with such noble force and carrying away all the debris. Restoring with unsurpassed purity. On this side of things, however, such is not meant to be permanent. We are not meant to remain. Those streams have momentum. They are meant to move us.

Thus, as consciousness returned him to the oblique state of things, as he was again feeling the sharp edges of more tortured questions without answers, he glanced over and saw the unopened box illuminated in the light of the pale moon streaming through his window. Pulling himself up, he opened it and found a letter that told the hauntingly beautiful story of Willie. Everything. From his orphaned childhood to the Bourby Gambit Guild, the encompassing shadows of the Deep Pen, Joe Wolf, Spamin Gruesome, and their nefarious plans, the Scallywags, and all the rest. All leading to his most triumphant moment in prison. A pawn for a king. Willie's tremendous sacrifice. *For him*.

For him. The thought began to ripple in the shallows, moving out and wide. But then it began moving down and deep. *For him*. His depths were being overtaken by a kind of mighty voice that could move mountains, before which he suddenly recognized that his place of prominence was not happenstance. Or fate. It was personal. And it was purposeful. *For him*.

Suddenly, he felt so small. Like a pawn. And yet, part of something so surpassingly great. A Kingdom.

The Do sat enveloped in unseen arms, holding the pawn as if it were the most priceless thing in the universe. He felt its weight. Greater than anything he'd ever accomplished or could possibly imagine. His Narcissyndrome mirror was summarily shattered. The ripples just kept rippling. So overwhelmed was he by awareness of this tiny little piglet's monumental heart, his total sacrifice *for him*, that he found himself consumed by a presence. With crystal clarity, he heard the Whisper speak: "You were there. As was I. And as I am now here. And will forever be."

Those streams from Great Silence must have overflowed their banks, as now The Do was experiencing them in a deluge of sobs he could not contain. A torrent from majestic falls meant to overflow into Pigletsville.

At this point, you surely know where this story is heading. Don Hairdo emerged all the more as the leader of Pigletsville, guiding the villagers to confront the evil forces of Spamin Gruesome and Deep Pen. He was fortified by the conviction that all political and social order is but an edifice rooted in timeless principles of goodness, beauty, and truth—the very fabric of the Whisper, a formidable foundation beneath the surface.

Peering into these depths, the real victory was realized in

return to unwavering attunement to the Whisper, awakened within them by the sweet *Ballad of Sagelia*, ennobling heroic hearts and illuminating the clear path, the most formidable weapons allowing them to defeat their adversaries and reclaim their beloved village.

As the resounding chorus of Squigglesprouts subsided in the splendor of the setting sun, a newfound sense of freedom and unity enveloped the community. Pigletsville was thriving again. While the defeat of Deep Pen and Spamin Gruesome was a cause for celebration, all knew that the battle against the shadows of Distraction and Disordered Desire had deep and formidable roots. Their tale was not yet complete. This was but the beginning of a new chapter of this eternal dance, demanding that they and future generations be ever more chiseled in virtue, drawing them into ever greater depths, with ever deeper conviction that they would one day find themselves not *Everywhere*, and certainly not *Anywhere*, but *Somewhere*, sails ever filled by the Whisper of the Unseen Someone.

HARROWING AWAKENING INTO THE GATHERING STORM

A midst the jubilant revelry that engulfed Pigletsville, concealed within the sinister embrace of the forest near Split Tree, Draven Blackclaw summoned the grim assembly to order. It was not defeat that loomed over them, but a festering seed of savage vengeance that thrived within their hopelessly splintered souls. And amidst the twisted throng of this clandestine gathering, there stood a figure, trembling under the weight of a stark revelation.

Concealed within the tumultuous chaos surrounding him, haunting memories clawed their way into his consciousness, transporting him back to a pivotal moment within the cold confines of New Pork Prison. Bound by duty to suppress the Syndicate's greatest fears, he had encountered an unexpected force—a purity so blinding, so profound, that it seared through the very essence of his being. It emanated from an insignificant figure known only as "Willie," whose singing of the haunting *Ballad of Sagelia* carried an inexplicable warmth that, from that day, had begun melting the icy tendrils of his soul.

With enlightenment came terror, as the veil of illusion was torn asunder, revealing the demonic machinations of Deep Pen. In a sudden, chilling realization, he understood that he was not the predator he had been led to believe, but rather a pawn ensnared in their web of deceit. Each shackle that fell away brought him face to face with the horrifying truth—he was Joe Piglet, a hapless puppet dangling from the clawed hands of their devilry.

Awakened to this harrowing truth of his nature, he knew his purpose with chilling clarity: to return to Pigletsville, burdened by the weight of remorse and armed with dire warnings. He would tread the treacherous path back to the heart of the hamlet, where the haunting melodies of the *Ballad of Sagelia* mingled with the almost celestial chorus of the Squigglesprouts, eclipsing every note of dread and despair. He must warn them of the dangers. He must join the fight with whatever semblance of life he had left within him. On the right side. Because he is a magnificent piglet. Breath of the Unseen Whisper. Made by Someone to journey forever deeper into the majestic depths of *Somewhere*.

At the crescendo of the terrifying ruckus, amid the inferno and echoing cries, Draven Blackclaw was arrested by a chilling intuition—a disturbance in the fiendish fabric of their clandestine world. His keen gaze pierced through the flames, catching sight of a familiar form disappearing into the enveloping shadows. A sinister transformation swept over his countenance; features contorted with demonic intensity. At that moment, a primal howl shattered the night, a deafening crescendo that echoed through the clearing, sending shivers down the spines of his minions and hushing even the most raucous among them—a portent of the ferocious battle yet to come.

From shallows into greater depths our greatest adventure awaits.

HAMLET HUDDLE:
Questions for Conversation

CHAPTER 1: Till Depth Do Us Part

WHAT STRUCK YOU, INSPIRED YOU, AND/OR CHALLENGED YOU?
WHAT QUESTIONS DID THIS CHAPTER RAISE?

1. In Pigletsville, depth is seen as an integral part of piglet existence, infused with empathy, trust, and genuine friendship. Discuss the significance of depth in fostering community and nurturing relationships. How does depth contribute to a sense of belonging and fulfillment?

2. The distinction between watchers, waders, treaders, swimmers, and divers highlights various approaches to interpersonal depth. Reflect on which category resonates with you the most and why. How do you navigate the complexities of social interactions and pursue deeper connections in your own life?

3. Divers are portrayed as individuals who exude quiet confidence and serve as safe harbors for others. Discuss the qualities that make a person a "diver" in the context of authentic friendship and trust. How can we cultivate these qualities within ourselves to become better friends and companions?

4. Willie's character exemplifies the value of persevering through trust fractures and remaining open to vulnerability in order to forge deep, meaningful connections. Share examples from your own life where perseverance and vulnerability led to the cultivation of authentic friendships. How can we overcome barriers to trust and embrace vulnerability in our relationships?

5. Reflect on the role of the Whisper of the Unseen in guiding the piglets toward deeper connections and a sense of transcendence. How does faith or spirituality influence your understanding of interpersonal depth and meaningful connections?

CHAPTER 2: THE BOURBY GAMBIT GUILD

WHAT STRUCK YOU, INSPIRED YOU, AND/OR CHALLENGED YOU?
WHAT QUESTIONS DID THIS CHAPTER RAISE?

1. Willie's character is depicted as unassuming yet deeply observant, finding joy in simple pleasures and moments of connection. Reflect on the importance of finding contentment and fulfillment amidst life's busyness.

2. The Bourby Gambit Guild serves as a haven for Willie, offering him a sense of belonging and camaraderie. Discuss the significance of friendship and community in fostering personal growth and resilience. How do Willie's interactions with the Bourbies shape his character and worldview?

3. Squigglesprout is described as a mystical floral wonder that hums melodically in proportion to sunlight, drawing others near with its infectious mirth. How are you like a Squigglesprout? How could you be more like a Squigglesprout? What difference would that make?

4. What parallels can be drawn between Squigglesprout's allure and the atmosphere of the Bourby Gambit Guild? Explore the role of laughter and joy in cultivating meaningful connections and enhancing one's sense of belonging.

5. Willie's journey from the sidelines to the heart of the Bourby Gambit Guild marks transformation from loneliness to a sense of purpose and belonging. Reflect on moments in your own life where stepping out of your comfort zone led to significant personal growth and new opportunities.

5. Thadeus McPorcinski's introduction to Willie highlights the warmth and camaraderie among the Bourbies, despite their playful banter and jovial demeanor. Discuss the importance of reaching out in fostering a welcoming community. How can we emulate the Bourbies' approach to friendship and hospitality in our own lives?

6. Bourbon is depicted as a symbol of camaraderie and celebration among the Bourby Gambit Guild. Reflect on the significance of shared rituals and traditions in strengthening social bonds and fostering a sense of belonging. How do shared experiences like enjoying a drink together contribute to the formation of lasting friendships?

CHAPTER 3: PAWN OF GREAT PRICE

WHAT STRUCK YOU, INSPIRED YOU, AND/OR CHALLENGED YOU?
WHAT QUESTIONS DID THIS CHAPTER RAISE?

1. Bourbon and chess are depicted as symbols of camaraderie and wisdom within the Bourby Gambit Guild. Discuss the significance of shared rituals and activities in fostering bonds of friendship and mutual understanding. How do shared interests and experiences contribute to a sense of belonging and acceptance?

2. Willie's initial perception of pawns as inconsequential accessories mirrors his own feelings of insignificance as a runt. Explore the symbolism of pawns in chess and their hidden capacity for transformation. How does Willie's realization of the pawn's supreme nobility parallel his own journey of self-discovery and acceptance?

3. McPorcinski's grandfatherly kindness and acceptance play a crucial role in Willie's integration into the Bourby Gambit Guild. Reflect on the importance of mentorship and guidance in fostering personal growth and resilience. How can acts of kindness and encouragement empower others to embrace their true worth and potential?

4. The Bourby Gambit Guild embodies a sense of belonging and camaraderie that, while anchored in fundamental truth, transcends individual differences and backgrounds. Discuss the qualities that make a community welcoming. How can we cultivate a sense of belonging in our own social circles and communities?

5. Reflect on the theme of sacrifice and transformation in Willie's journey and the role it plays in shaping his character. How do moments of sacrifice and selflessness contribute to personal growth and the strengthening of relationships? Share examples from your own life where acts of sacrifice led to positive outcomes or deeper connections with others.

CHAPTER 4: INCONSPICUOUS SAGE IN PUBLIC SQUARE

WHAT STRUCK YOU, INSPIRED YOU, AND/OR CHALLENGED YOU?
WHAT QUESTIONS DID THIS CHAPTER RAISE?

1. Willie's interactions with Mr. Snodberry demonstrate his ability to navigate complex topics with wisdom and insight. Reflect on a time when you engaged in a thought-provoking conversation with someone whose perspective challenged your own. How did the exchange shape your understanding of the topic or your own beliefs?

2. In the dialogue between Willie and Mr. Snodberry, Willie often responds to questions with philosophical reflections. Discuss the role of philosophical inquiry in fostering deeper understanding and critical thinking. How can engaging in philosophical discussions enrich our lives and relationships?

3. Despite his humble role as a paperboy, Willie remains steadfast in his commitment to truth and clarity. Reflect on the importance of integrity and authenticity in maintaining one's sense of self amidst societal pressures and expectations. How can we cultivate a strong sense of identity and purpose regardless of our circumstances?

4. Willie's approach to conversations differs from those who seek validation through conformity. Explore the concept of intellectual independence and the courage required to challenge prevailing opinions and beliefs. How can we cultivate the confidence to express our own perspectives authentically while remaining open to diverse viewpoints?

5. As Willie engages in discussions with Mr. Snodberry, he demonstrates the capacity to inspire others to think deeply about complex issues. Reflect on the influence of individuals who embody wisdom and clarity in their interactions with others. How can we cultivate these qualities within ourselves to positively impact those around us?

6. Consider the metaphor of the newsstand as a stage where wisdom and curiosity waltz together. Reflect on the role of dialogue and exchange of ideas in shaping our understanding of the world. How can we create spaces for meaningful conversations that promote mutual respect, empathy, and intellectual growth?

CHAPTER 5: The Ballad of Sagelia

What struck you, inspired you, and/or challenged you? What questions did this chapter raise?

1. The *Ballad of Sagelia* portrays themes of selflessness, sacrifice, and the battle between light and darkness. Reflect on a character or event from literature, mythology, or history that embodies similar themes. How does the tale of *Sagelia* resonate with other stories of heroism and redemption?

2. Sagelia possesses the gift of insight into the nature of Distraction, enabling her to see through deception and guide her fellow piglets back to the path of purpose. Discuss the significance of that gift and its relevance to navigating moral dilemmas and challenges in your life.

3. Divertusis represents the allure of temptation and the dangers of succumbing to selfishness and entitlement. Reflect on a time when you or someone you know faced similar temptations or encountered individuals who exploited others for their own gain. How did you navigate the situation, and what lessons did you learn?

4. Sagelia's ultimate sacrifice highlights the power of selflessness and the willingness to confront evil at great personal cost. Discuss the impact of Sagelia's actions on the piglet community and the enduring legacy of her bravery. How does Sagelia's story inspire you to consider the greater good and act with courage in your own life?

5. The *Ballad of Sagelia* emphasizes the importance of remaining attuned to the guiding principles of unity, kindness, and moral clarity embodied by the Whisper. Reflect on the values that guide your own life and the role of community in upholding shared virtues. How can we cultivate a sense of moral integrity and responsibility in our communities?

6. Consider the role of myths and legends in shaping cultural identity and transmitting moral teachings across generations. How do stories like the *Ballad of Sagelia* contribute to the cultural heritage of Pigletsville and reinforce shared values and beliefs? How can we draw inspiration from them to address contemporary challenges and promote positive personal, familial, communal and global change?

CHAPTER 6: THE MALPHAS MEMO: SIZZILIAN PROTOCOL

WHAT STRUCK YOU, INSPIRED YOU, AND/OR CHALLENGED YOU?
WHAT QUESTIONS DID THIS CHAPTER RAISE?

Memo 1: The Broad Stroke

1. Discuss: "Through its gradual infiltration and corruption, sacred boundaries once unquestioned... will become curiosities. Curiosities will become options; options will transform into offerings; offerings will evolve into commonplace; and the commonplace will evolve into institutional obligation, encroaching upon every aspect of piglet life!"

2. How does seduction, the graduality of manipulation, resonate with experiences of temptation or moral compromise in your own life? What were the underlying motivations or influences behind these actions?

3. Discuss the prominent influencers in your life and the world today, particularly the media. Are they accurate? Do people generally approach them critically? What's at stake?

4. In what ways can we guard against the gradual erosion of moral integrity in the face of pressures or temptations?

5. How can self-awareness help us recognize the subtle signs of moral compromise or manipulation in our lives, enabling us to resist and maintain our integrity?

Memo 2: Descent into Desolation

1. Discuss: "What grand amusemen... these pitiful creatures waving banners of 'tolerance' with such sanctimonious fervor, selectively applying it to that which is *ours*, bad and false, while remaining *intolerant* of that which is good and true! Oblivious to the truth that if words can mean anything, they lose all meaning. And in that void, everything becomes ours to manipulate and control."

2. Discuss: "We will hide behind inane, dismissive pronouncements sewn in their pathetic piglet souls, such as 'your truth' and 'who are you to say,' as if the entire landscape of existence is a plaything of their passion! 'Who dares to judge?' [will silence] dissent with the chilling comfort of ambiguity."

3. How can we discern truth amidst the noise of subjective interpretations and feelings? How can we cultivate inner clarity and discernment to resist these tactics?

Memo 3: Casting Hurls Before Swine

1. Discuss: "Why, my pernicious pupil, at every step along the perilous path of seduction we will anesthetize them with just the right whisper! Just the right amount of distraction! For instance, as those insufferable notes of the *Ballad* may spark, reaching up from sacred depths we have yet to tarnish, we douse them with dismissal: 'Don't be silly! It's a phantom memory! A fleeting sentiment! A thing of fairytales! Something thoroughly unreliable!' This is best followed up by ingratiating their egos, 'You're much more clever!'

2. Reflecting on your own experiences, can you recall a time when you felt the pangs associated with realizing you were off track morally or spiritually? How did you respond, and what lessons did you learn from that experience?

3. Reflect on instances where you have witnessed or experienced the rejection of truth and goodness in favor of personal desires or ideologies. What were the consequences?

4. Discuss the how shame, contempt and animosity can hold us captive. How can these be recognized and averted?

5. How can cultivating virtues such as humility, honesty, and integrity help us resist manipulation and deception, enabling us to live truth and goodness in the face of adversity?

CHAPTER 7: BATTLE AGAINST DARKNESS

WHAT STRUCK YOU, INSPIRED YOU, AND/OR CHALLENGED YOU?
WHAT QUESTIONS DID THIS CHAPTER RAISE?

1. In the face of overwhelming darkness and deception, Willie undergoes a profound transformation marked by awakening to the prevalence of the Grip in his interior life, an unseen spiritual power against which he exercises his authority and banishes It. Have you felt similar forces holding you captive? Consider taking authority over them by identifying them by name, banishing them, and inviting the Whisper of the Unseen.

Some examples: Lust, Addiction, Rejection, Deception, Anxiety, Fear, Deceit, Anger, Blame, Failure, Control.

2. The imagery of Willie standing at the summit, liberated from the Grip, symbolizes a profound sense of freedom and clarity. Discuss the significance of self-discovery and self-acceptance in achieving personal growth and fulfillment. How can individuals embrace their past experiences and vulnerabilities as sources of strength rather than sources of shame or limitation?

3. McPorcinski's mentorship and guidance play a pivotal role in Willie's journey toward self-realization. Reflect on the importance of mentorship and supportive relationships in fostering personal development and resilience. How can individuals seek out and nurture meaningful connections that empower them to overcome adversity and pursue their goals?

4. Willie's experience of tapping into a deeper source of wisdom and guidance suggests a spiritual dimension to his journey of self-discovery. Reflect on the role of spirituality reflection in navigating life's challenges and finding meaning and purpose. How can individuals cultivate a deeper connection to their the Whisper of the Unseen to foster resilience and well-being?

CHAPTER 8: ECHOES OF SILENCE

WHAT STRUCK YOU, INSPIRED YOU, AND/OR CHALLENGED YOU?
WHAT QUESTIONS DID THIS CHAPTER RAISE?

1. In this chapter, Willie finds solace and strength, his identity and mission, symbolized by a solitary pawn. Reflect on the significance of symbols in literature and life, and how they can serve as powerful reminders of one's values, beliefs, and purpose.

2. Willie's silent plea for guidance reflects the universal human experience of grappling with uncertainty and seeking direction in times of turmoil. Discuss the role of introspection and spiritual inquiry in navigating life's challenges and finding meaning and purpose. How can individuals cultivate a sense of guidance and resilience in the face of uncertainty?

3. Despite the absence of a discernible reply from the Whisper, Willie remains committed to his daily rituals and expressions of faith. Reflect on the theme of faith and perseverance in the absence of immediate answers or tangible signs of guidance. How can individuals sustain their faith and commitment to their beliefs during times of doubt or uncertainty? What strategies or practices can individuals employ to maintain hope and motivation during difficult times?

4. Willie's sense of being a "cog in the wheel" and witnessing cherished truths crumbling under the influence of external forces highlights the theme of disillusionment and existential crisis. Discuss the challenges of maintaining integrity and authenticity in a world characterized by deception and manipulation. How can individuals reconcile their personal values with the pressures of societal expectations?

5. The chapter portrays Willie's ongoing struggle to connect with the Whisper and receive guidance in the midst of uncertainty. Reflect on the theme of spiritual communication and the quest for inner wisdom. How do individuals discern and interpret signs or messages from sources beyond their immediate perception? What practices or rituals can facilitate a deeper connection to one's inner guidance?

CHAPTER 9: RISE OF THE SHATTERGLASS SCALLYWAGS

WHAT STRUCK YOU, INSPIRED YOU, AND/OR CHALLENGED YOU?
WHAT QUESTIONS DID THIS CHAPTER RAISE?

1. The Scallywags' gatherings serve as a sanctuary for piglets seeking refuge from the pervasive darkness of Deep Pen's influence. Discuss the role of missioned community and mutual support in providing resilience and hope during times of crisis. What would such a community look like meriting your engagement?

2. The naming of the Shatterglass Scallywags reflects their identity and mission: To shatter the illusions propagated by Deep Pen and reclaim the truth. It derives organically from their common connection to the *Ballad* flowing into friendship, and simply sharing life together. How important are common, defining stories that anchor our lives in spiritual identity, purpose, depth and scope? What impactful stories and rituals give you purpose? How might you more fully tap those streams with your family and friends?

3. Willie's decision to embark on a perilous journey to *New Pork* in search of The Do demonstrates his courage and commitment. Reflect on the theme of heroism and sacrifice in life. What qualities and actions define a hero? How are you called to be a hero right now? What will that take? What stands in the way? What help do you need to overcome?

4. The enigmatic figure of The Do represents a beacon of hope amidst the darkness of Deep Pen's influence, even with his notable flaws. Who or what has inspired you with the possibility of transformation and redemption?

5. Reflect on the theme of sacrifice and selflessness in the pursuit of justice and freedom. Who has demonstrated to you courage and resilience in the face of danger, and what lessons can be drawn from them?

CHAPTER 10: UNSEEN CLASH OF SWORDS

WHAT STRUCK YOU, INSPIRED YOU, AND/OR CHALLENGED YOU?
WHAT QUESTIONS DID THIS CHAPTER RAISE?

1. The confrontation between Draven Blackclaw and Joe Wolf reveals a power struggle within the ranks of the Deep Pen Syndicate. How do leaders like Draven Blackclaw exploit fear and uncertainty to consolidate their power and suppress dissent?

2. Beyond physical apprehension, Draven Blackclaw senses a "disturbance" in the atmosphere. Do we have that "spiritual" sense? Have you ever experienced it? Can you share any examples? How might such a sensibility be cultivated and exercised for the good of others? What might be some healthy considerations?

3. Joe Wolf's uneasy demeanor and assurance to redouble efforts highlight the pressure and responsibility placed on those tasked with maintaining order and control on behalf of oppressive regimes. Discuss the moral dilemmas faced by individuals in such situations. How do they reconcile their loyalty to their leaders with their own conscience and sense of right and wrong?

4. The ominous warning from Draven Blackclaw underscores the seriousness of the perceived threat to the Deep Pen Syndicate's plans. Reflect on the theme of paranoia and insecurity among oppressive regimes. How do leaders like Draven Blackclaw respond to perceived threats to their power, and what measures do they take to maintain their control?

5. The clandestine nature of the Deep Pen Syndicate's operations and the use of covert agents to suppress dissent raise questions about surveillance and surveillance states. Reflect on the implications of widespread surveillance and the erosion of privacy rights in authoritarian societies. How do surveillance tactics contribute to the consolidation of power and the suppression of opposition voices?

CHAPTER 11: ESCAPE TO NEW PORK

WHAT STRUCK YOU, INSPIRED YOU, AND/OR CHALLENGED YOU?
WHAT QUESTIONS DID THIS CHAPTER RAISE?

1. Explore the significance of Willie's dreams as he journeys towards New Pork. How do his dreams reflect his inner turmoil, fears, and hopes? What themes or motifs emerge from the dream sequences, and how do they contribute to the overall narrative? Have you had any consequential dreams?

2. Discuss the role of McPorcinski in Willie's journey. How does their meeting provide comfort and guidance to Willie amidst his struggles? Discuss the importance of familial connections and unexpected allies in times of crisis.

3. Reflect on Willie's reaction upon reading the damning headline in the *New Pork Times*. How does the portrayal of Willie as a "dangerous terrorist" challenge a reader's perception of his character? Has your character been unfairly colored? Have you contributed to the same for others?

4. How does the pawn serve as a symbol of stength, friendship, and determination? Discuss the role of cherished memories and tokens in sustaining hope and guiding one's actions in the face of adversity.

5. Consider the implications of The Do's presence in New Pork and Willie's determination to reach him. How does the revelation of The Do's incarceration impact Willie's mission and the broader struggle against Deep Pen?

6. Discuss Willie's transformation from a state of despair to one of renewed determination. What was consequential for Willie's internal awakening and journey?

CHAPTER 12: THE WEIGHT OF SHADOWS

WHAT STRUCK YOU, INSPIRED YOU, AND/OR CHALLENGED YOU?
WHAT QUESTIONS DID THIS CHAPTER RAISE?

1. Explore the significance of Willie's dreams as he journeys towards New Pork. How do his dreams reflect his inner turmoil, fears, and hopes? What themes or motifs emerge from the dream sequences, and how do they contribute to the overall narrative? Have you had any consequential dreams?

2. Discuss the role of McPorcinski in Willie's journey. How does their meeting provide comfort and guidance to Willie amidst his struggles? Discuss the importance of familial connections and unexpected allies in times of crisis.

3. Reflect on Willie's reaction upon reading the damning head-line in the *New Pork Times*. How does the portrayal of Willie as a "dangerous terrorist" challenge a reader's perception of his character? Has your character been unfairly colored? Have you contributed to the same for others?

4. How does the pawn serve as a symbol of stength, friendship, and determination? Discuss the role of cherished memories and tokens in sustaining hope and guiding one's actions in the face of adversity.

5. Consider the implications of The Do's presence in New Pork and Willie's determination to reach him. How does the revelation of The Do's incarceration impact Willie's mission and the broader struggle against Deep Pen?

6. Discuss Willie's transformation from a state of despair to one of renewed determination. What was consequential for Willie's internal awakening and journey?

CHAPTER 13: PAWN OF GREAT POWER

WHAT STRUCK YOU, INSPIRED YOU, AND/OR CHALLENGED YOU?
WHAT QUESTIONS DID THIS CHAPTER RAISE?

1. How does the pawn represent Willie's identity, resilience, and sacrifice? Discuss the significance of the pawn as a symbol of hope, transformation, and ultimate selflessness in Willie's journey.

2. Reflect on the power of music in Chapter 13. How does Willie's singing of the *Ballad of Sagelia* transcend the physical confines of his prison cell, inspiring hope and unity among his fellow inmates? Discuss the transformative effect of music on souls. What songs have made a difference in your life?

3. Discuss the themes of sacrifice and redemption in Chapter 13. How does Willie's ultimate sacrifice for the greater good exemplify a surpassing power, the depths of love, character, and what really matters? How does such selfishness inspire transformation in the hearts of those around us? How has such forged the things we now cherish? What are some opportunities we have every day to cultivate such character?

4. Consider the allegorical elements and social commentary present in Chapter 13. How does Willie's journey parallel real-world struggles against oppression, manipulation, and propaganda? Discuss the broader implications of Willie's story in addressing themes of resistance, perseverance, and the pursuit of truth in the face of tyranny.

5. Have you ever been struck by something that inspired solemn reverence? Do you believe there is unseen power beyond what the visible world wields? What is it?

6. What is the capacity of great art to forge our souls for transcendent beauty, to connect with the divine? What are examples in your life? How are you like a Squigglesprout?

CHAPTER 14: THE TORCH IS PASSED

WHAT STRUCK YOU, INSPIRED YOU, AND/OR CHALLENGED YOU?
WHAT QUESTIONS DID THIS CHAPTER RAISE?

1. Can you relate to the transformation of Don Hairdo? What was most consequential? Have similar moments played out in your life? What spiritual or emotional challenges have you overcome? Tell your story.

2. Do our physical lives reveal something of our souls? How so or not? What does the over-the-top literary description of The Do's mane punctuate about the reality of external expression. What do your choices in physical appearance and mannerisms say about you? What would you like them to say about you?

3. How does The Do's struggle with Narcissyndrome hinder his ability to challenge Deep Pen's manipulation and oppression? Analyze how adversity serves as a catalyst for The Do's personal growth and moral development, leading to his emergence as a steadfast leader. Can you relate?

4. How does the *Ballad* awaken clarity and resolve within The Do, prompting him to challenge the Grip? Discuss the transformative impact of music and ancestral wisdom in guiding The Do towards his greater self.

5. How does The Do's resilience and determination in the face of Deep Pen's attacks speak to you about the capacity to inspire hope and unity? Do you have that in you? Would you like that more in you? What would that take? What stands in the way? What help do you need?

CHAPTER 15: A TALE OF TRIUMPH

WHAT STRUCK YOU, INSPIRED YOU, AND/OR CHALLENGED YOU? WHAT QUESTIONS DID THIS CHAPTER RAISE?

1. Reflect on the pivotal role of Willie's sacrifice and the revelation of his story to The Do in Chapter 15. How does Willie's journey, from orphaned childhood to his heroic sacrifice, serve as a catalyst for The Do's profound transformation? Discuss the significance of The Do's emotional response to Willie's sacrifice and its impact on his leadership.

2. Discuss the ultimate confrontation between Pigletsville and the forces of Deep Pen, led by Spamin Gruesome. How does the victory over Deep Pen symbolize the triumph of good over evil, fueled by the collective awakening inspired by Sagelia's *Ballad*? Discuss the themes of unity, courage, and resilience that contribute to Pigletsville's success in reclaiming their village.

3. Discuss the role of the Whisper, the essence of the timeless principles of truth, beauty, and goodness, in guiding Pigletsville towards victory. How does the community's attunement to the Whisper empower them to confront adversity and resist the manipulative tactics of Deep Pen? Discuss the transformative impact of embracing the Whisper on both individual characters and the collective community.

4. Consider the concluding sentiments of Chapter 15, emphasizing the ongoing struggle against the shadows of Distraction and Disordered Desire. How does the recognition of this eternal struggle underscore the importance of humility and vigilance in maintaining Pigletsville's newfound freedom and unity? Discuss the implications of this realization for the characters as they embark on a new chapter in their journey.

5. Discuss the transformative power of sacrifice and redemption in shaping the destiny of Pigletsville and its inhabitants.

6. Explore the concept of the eternal dance depicted in Chapter 15, the nature of struggle and redemption in our personal and corporate ongoing quest for truth. How does this metaphor encapsulate the enduring journey of Pigletsville and its inhabitants?

EPILOGUE: HARROWING AWAKENING TO THE GATHERING STORM

WHAT STRUCK YOU, INSPIRED YOU, AND/OR CHALLENGED YOU?
WHAT QUESTIONS DID THIS CHAPTER RAISE?

1. Reflecting on Joe Wolf's journey from ignorance to enlightenment, have you ever experienced a moment of profound realization that shattered your previous perceptions or beliefs? How did this revelation impact your understanding of yourself and the world around you?

2. Joe Wolf grapples with the realization that he has been a pawn in the Syndicate's sinister schemes. Have you ever felt manipulated or deceived by external forces or ideologies? How did you respond to this realization, and what steps did you take to reclaim your autonomy and agency?

3. The haunting melodies of the *Ballad of Sagelia* serve as a beacon of hope amidst the chaos and despair of Pigletsville. Can you recall a time when music or art played a significant role in guiding you through difficult circumstances or inspiring you to pursue virtue and truth?

4. Joe Wolf's transformation from predator to protector underscores the theme of redemption and the capacity for change within every individual. Reflecting on your own experiences, have you ever witnessed or undergone a transformation that allowed you to embrace a new identity or purpose? What lessons did you learn from this journey of self-discovery?

5. The revelation of Joe Wolf's true identity as a piglet raises questions about the nature of our authentic identity and mission in life. Is our identity really something we can determine, or is it something in which we are determined? Can any identity surpass that of forged by the Whisper for life in the Whisper? How does Animas Aberratus mitigate against our identity? Why? How can we stand?and conflicts that lie ahead for the characters?

6. As Joe Wolf embarks on his journey back to Pigletsville, burdened by remorse and armed with dire warnings, he grapples with the concept of moral responsibility. How do you define moral responsibility, and what role does it play in shaping your decisions and actions? What is the importance and value of "turning" from darkness to light, and how is this accomplished through authentic apology and forgiveness?

ACKNOWLEDGMENTS

I am immensely grateful for the attentive and expert editing of Erin Broestl, whose professional affirmation early on confirmed that this story was impactful and powerful, worthy of being told.

I extend abundant gratitude to my amazing writer friends who provided wonderful support and helpful feedback throughout the process: Jeff Barefoot, Joe Campo, Faith Hough, Jonathan Jakubowski, Jim Lange, Fr. Darrin Merlino, Kathryn Nelson, Liz Strang, and Jennifer Wagner. I must add a shout-out to a special intercessor friend, Nicholas Smith.

If I endeavored to name all the truly remarkable family and friends throughout the years who have constituted my own Bourby Gambit Guild and Shatterglass Scallywags, I would inadvertently miss someone. You know who you are. Your friendship, support, love and prayers have sustained me. You mean everything. You are in this. I'm beyond blessed to be *in* this very real journey with you along the path toward that incredible *Somewhere*.

My beloved children, my Squigglesprouts, this story is, above all, my share in the unsurpassed heart, hope, and promise the Whisper of the Unseen has for each of you, reverberating to each of your children down through generations. You were made for magnificence. May my ceiling be your floor.

Stephanie, my beloved best friend and wife of over 25 years, you have pored over these pages and endured my often way-too-early writing promptings with unwavering patience and support. You are the Quintessential Squigglesprout. Beyond words, I love you.

And above all, my ineffable acknowledgment, esteem and adoration to the Holy Trinity, the Whisper of the Unseen, in and through Whom all is created and held in existence. Keep summoning us, guiding us, and drawing us ever deeper into Your Depths.

AUTHOR

GREG SCHLUETER is a media producer, author, radio show host, and movement leader fostering the convivial friendship of the Bourbies, passionate pursuit of the Scallywags, and the overall vibrant culture of Pigletsville. He lives in Holland, Ohio, with his wife, Stephanie, where they lead a movement committed to Someone leading us *Somewhere* guided by the Whisper of the Unseen. They are parents of seven with an ever-growing number of little Squigglesprouts.

Enter the enchanting world of Squigglesprout.com.
Find out more about their movement at ILoveMyFamily.us.
Listen to their weekly radio program and
podcast at IGNITERadioLive.com.
Follow Greg on Substack at GregorianRant.us.

PUBLISHER

SQUIGGLESPROUT is a media company founded in 2024. Our mission is to open souls to the horizon of the Good, Beautiful, True, and One through magnificent storytelling.

BLOOMiNATION. Bloom + Illumination + Nation.

"[A] word on Squigglesprout, the most enchanting floral wonder in all the world. In proportion to the sunlight bathing its delicate form, the mystical blue Squigglesprout hums a melodic tune which, amid its august company on a radiant summer day, becomes a chorus reverberating through the air. Each of its leaflets seems to sway in rhythm, adding a whimsical ballet to the garden's ensemble. Its sprightly nature draws others near, inviting them to partake in its infectious mirth."

- The Magnificent Piglets of Pigletsville

www.ingramcontent.com/pod-product-compliance
Lightning Source LLC
Chambersburg PA
CBHW020626130626
46552CB00003B/1104